MAMA AMERICA

AZUKA MONYEI

CONTENTS

CHAPTER ONE

Ajulu had a perculiar humble beginning. Her parents Ogadi and Asia wallowed in abject poverty which many believed to all and Sundry in Akado, an agrarian Community, to be self - inflicted.

At the age of ten, Ajulu was given out to Nene as housemaid. Nene otherwise called Alhaja or Mama Kano was a strong community woman. Many did not know that despite Nene's mode of dressing that made her appear like a Muslim and her fluency in Hausa language she was neither a Muslim by faith nor had she ever gone on pilgrimage to Mecca. Nevertheless, Nene had lived in the city of Kano for thirty eight years. AIhaja Nene was a successful Palm Oil dealer who had tens of distribution outlets across Kano State. She was mother figure to all who came from Akado and neighbouring villages residing in the city of Kano. It was said that Nene's kind disposition toward the needy and poor was unequalled.

Alhaja Nene fled kano a city she had seen as her second home following a religious crisis that erupted in the city. She virtually lost everything as her personal house and many shops were vandalized and burnt down.

Alhaja Nene courageously put her pieces together as quickly as she arrive her native community. Ajulu's coming to live with her gave her great joy. Ajulu proved to be obedient and hard working. Even at her tender age she was at home with house chores. She prepared tasty meals to the admiration of all.

Nene began to treat her as an adopted child. She showed Ajulu love and care. Nene did not believe in the education of a girl child otherwise she would have sent her to school like her peers in the community. This was why all appeals by Ajulu that she should be allowed to go to school fell on deaf ears. Nene preferred to teach her the act of soap making, weaving and dyeing of cloths. Also, Ajulu assisted Nene in her vegetable farm. They were enveloped in hard work her mates in the neighbourhood. Ajulu grew up to be kind to all who came her way.

Nene's sudden death left Ajulu in deep shock, disbelief and pain. Ajulu recalled that on the night Nene died in her sleep; hours before she went to bed she had told members of her household what appeared to be her life history with particular emphasis on her friendship with Folashade, Amina, Saudat and Ngozi. Nene paid glowing tributes to Alhaji Yusuf Kano, her companion of thirty five year. Nene addressed a personal issue agitating peoples mind as to why she remained single all her life. She told all seated in her living room that her inability to get married was caused by challenges inflicted on her by her Marine husband'. This she claimed was privilege information she got from some 'men of God'. She regretted that these spiritual men fought tooth and nail to reverse the condition to no avail. A thoroughly shocked audience pitifully saw reason why a very beautiful and elegant woman as Nene remained a spinster at sixty two. Nene's emotional laden voice attracted empathy to her. Nduka, Nene's age mate and first cousin took Nene's story with a pinch of salt. He recalled that as teenagers, Nene was notoriously wayward. She eloped with a man at nineteen only to resurface nine years later after subjecting her mother, relations and friends to unbearable trauma. It was during this period Nene's mother died and many were quick to attribute her death to the heartache Nene caused her.

Nduka chose to maintain dignified silence and not to open the can of worms on Nene's indecent past.

Nene's further lamented that she was broke. She recounted how virtually all her property in Kano were destroyed by some religious zealots bringing her to her knees. She rained curses on whoever had a hand in the destruction of her property, all she worked for on earth.

Many were rudely shocked when Nene was found stone dead on her 7″ by 6″ wooden bed the following morning. Ajulu remembered with fondness the nice times she had with the deceased woman who treated her like a beloved daughter. To her, a mother had passed on. She cried her eyes out.

As quickly as Nene's funeral ceremony was over, Ajulu went back to her parents' house. Though she was happy to be home, her feeling was thinned out by the day by the grinding poverty ravaging her family. The family virtually relied on the meager income Asia realized from sales of firewood. Neighbours were at a lost as to why Ogadi could not fend for his family. Ogadi had a farm but yet no farm. His farm was always over run by weeds. Palm wine was soul mate.

Asia would not forget in a hurray how Ogadi in his sleep was punching someone whom he accused of throwing away some two day old palm wine he requested should be reserved for him.

"What nonsense are you talking about? How dare you, a mere bar attendant throw away a two day palm wine I specially asked your Madam to keep for me. Don't you know it'd be mature for good enjoyment? You fool! You never-do-well. You .... You .... "Ogadi, choked with anger barked throwing some punches in the air. "Who are you releasing punches on? Why do you make a mountain out of every issue pertaining to palm wine? May God deliver you from this bondage!" Asia who lay beside her husband blurted out visibly boiling on the inside.

"Abomination!Woman, who gave you the audacity to chastise me, your husband. I mean, a man who paid your bride prize. You had better keep your tongue in cheek or else….." Ogadi roared. An intimidated Asia maintained her peace. In a few moments Ogadi snored away. For Asia, sleep took a flight. A mist tears, she wondered why fate purnished her with Ogadi.

Moment by moment, Ajulu was saddened that her father had become a prisoner to alcohol. Her heart bled and almost burst on the occasion her father, Ogadi was brought back home from the Palm wine joint in a wheel barrow.

Ogadi gave poverty as the reason for his heavy drinking habit. "Why do people judge me harshly? Ogadi asked Ndu, a relation who came to advise him to set himself free from the grip of alcohol and embrace hard work.

"In the face of my present economic difficulties, I find solace in palm wine. It has proved to be my reliable ally. It's my best friend! "Ogadi had lamented.

"But you've got large uncultivated farm land that could be enough for five able bodied men to farm. Why would you not till the land and provide for your family. My brother, embrace hard work and save your family from starvation and shame," Ndu insisted.

"I hear you! It's farm! Farm!! Farm!!! Your usual sing – song! Does farming not amount to suffering? Aren't you tired of suffering? I'm sure someone left his brain at home. Enough of this un-solicited advice." Ogadi charged.

"Well! I'm taking my leave now but let heaven and earth bear witness that I gave you sincere and brotherly advice. And all I get for it was insult. On a final note, let me remind you that your solace in al-cohol is most embarrassing and self-destructive".

"Leave! And leave now! Sincere and brotherly advice my foot! Go and first manage your fam-ily challenges before you think of whom to advice. After all, who does not know in Akado Community that your talkative wife, Unoju is a cheap gossip and wayward.

CHAPTER TWO

kunne palm wine bar was clearly the most popular in Akado. It was situated at the bubbling market square. Many palm wine drinkers believed that Akunne sold the finest palm wine in the community. Also, she prepared delicious goat and bush meat pepper soup, a delicacy that go with palm wine.

Ogadi and friends, regular callers at the bar, from 6.30am, customers begin to assemble at the palm wine bar. They drink till 12mid night when Akume closed her business for the day. A few were relunctant to go home.

Ogadi never considered any day as good unless he visited Akunne palm wine bar. Regardless of the huge credit he had accumulated, the bar never missed his daily presence. At the bar, news was virtually distorted and dish out. Rumours and gossips were traded and private lives of successful individuals in society formed topical issues for discussion. Perceived failures were murdered with tongue, chewed and spat out. Akunne's palm wine bar was the place to be for breaking news on marriage and divorces, births, deaths and burials. Also, the thoughts, plans and actions of important people in the community were laid bare at the palm wine joint. Most customers at the bar were all knowing and all-wise.

Ogadi came back one fateful day at the dead of the night dead drunk. As hungry as a wolf, he requested for his dinner from his wife who has been awake anxiously awaiting his return. Asia told Ogadi point blank that there was no food noting that she small piece of yam left in the house was boiled for the children for dinner. But Ogadi would hear of it.

"What nonsense are you talking about? You mean that there is no food for me in my own house? You mean that there is no food for the head of the family. What an insult of the highest order and from a lazy woman. Anyway, I'd not take it from you. You had better go bring my food or I'd cause hell to crash on your head," Ogadi screeched.

"Well! I'm sorry. But I don't know where to get you food. I've been doing my possible best to provide food for the family. I deserve commendation. I wish that I'm getting some support from you no matter how little," Asia replied in great fright. "Oh! Oh!! Oh!!! Asia, you're insinuating I'm useless and irresponsible. What an insult from an ungrateful woman I married with my hard earned money."

"Which hard earned money are you talking about? Who does not know in Akado Community that your late father bore the cost of our marriage ceremony."

"Which my father? I ask which my father bore the cost of our marriage ceremony. I knew it. Yes! I knew that your warped mind has failed to re-call that I've always been a successful farmer. You always create the cloud I'm nobody.

Anyway, we'd know who is the head of this family today."

"I hear…… hear you! Successful….Successful farmer indeed! Yet you can't feed your ……"

Before Asia could land, Ogadi pounced on her with fury. He threw punches and kicked Asia who was down on the floor.

"You're a beast! You're beast! You're……. Real men don't beat women. To do so is to live below the level of a real man," Asia yelled.

Asia's cry attracted neighbours to the scene. A rattled and hepless Ajulu cried with her siblings. They shed tears in solidarity with their agonizing mother.

At the break, Diokpa Chukwuma, the head of Ogadi's extended family summoned a meeting to settle the quarrel between Ogadi and Asia despite Nwizu's strenuous protest, the meeting warned Asia to desist from insulting her husband. They told her to respect her husband unconditionally. Asia was asked to kneel down and tender an unqualified apology to Ogadi for insinuating he was a lazy man.

Asia tearfully fell on her knees and apologized profusely to her husband. She recalled being advisedly warned by an aunty that no wife wins her husband in a matter brought before his kinsmen. According to the elderly woman, where that was about to happen, the man would resort to the use of blackmail to turn the tide against his wife.

Asia my daughter, let sleeping dog lie. Go home and prepare Ogadi's best meal for him that peace my reign supreme in your family,"Diokpa Chukwuma said.

As quickly as Asia left the meeting, Nwizu stated that they owe Ogadi a moral responsibility to impress it on him to strive to support his family.

"Let the antelope help and let the elephant help to urge our brother Ogadi to embrace hard work and severe the company of slots, never-do-wells and the ungodly. Let the truth be told, Asia was right. Our own dear brother is less than a man," Nwizu posited.

"I'd not give cedit to your ill remark. Everyone knows you hate me and even wish me dead," Ogadi uncouthly and swiftly retorted.

Ogadi had not farmed for four years. Shortly before he abandoned farming, he had complained to Ezeife, a notorious community loafer that for two

years running, termites had over run his farm causing serious damage to his crops. Ezeife was quick tell
Ogadi that he had, had similar painful experience
in the past. He stated that when all effort to arrest
the situation failed, he was compelled to consult the
oracle who revealed that their gods of the fathers
had banned him from doing any farm work. He advisedly warned Ogadi to toe his line or face dire
consequences. "For this singular reason, my loving
and understanding wives provide for all my needs at
moment."

Ogadi looked forward to leaving the farm for
good and quickly too. The opportunity presented it-
self when on one occasion Ogaid went to the farm
and ran into an antelope held by his trap. The animal
was the biggest Ogadi had set eyes on. The antelope
was full of life. It was held weakly by a tiny wire that
was joined to a rope and then to a long stick. The
animal had been struggling to gain its freedom to no
avail.

Gazing at the prized animal, Ogadi steamed
in joy speakable. Hugging himself and beating his
chest in self congratulation, Ogadi shot out.

"On you, I'll settle my debt in Akunne's palm
wine bar; buy a new bicycle; buy wrapper for Nkiru
my darling concubine. On you….. Oh! On you, I'll…..
I'll…."

An excited Ogadi danced to an inaudible
music for moments. He raised his glittering cutlass
and hurriedly made to strike the animal's head but

the giant antelope took a dock. Ogadi inadvertently cut the rope holding the wire that held the animal captive setting it free.

In a flash, the antelope with the speed of light melted into the bush. Standing like a statue, Ogadi was speechless. With hands akimbo, grief and confusion clouded him. Moments later, Ogadi left the farm dejected. On his way home, he greeted no one nor answered greetings from natives he met on the foot path to the farm. At home he yelled at his children for no just cause. That Ogadi boiled on the inside all day was an understatement.

Recounting his sad story at Akunne's palm wine bar, Ezeife who had been enjoying himself having deceived one of his wives into parting with some money wasted no time in reminding a heart-broken Ogadi to harken to the voice of the gods before he attracted to himself their wrath.

"What further evidence do you need to prove that the gods of our land have banished you from the farm? Be warned not to attract their wrath to yourself and your family because the dire consequence is better imagined."

With that stern warning, Ogadi resolved never to set his foot on the farm. He was quick to announce to his family and relations that the oracle had banned him from going to the farm. "The oracle has spoken." Ogadi told any person who cared to listen. However, he failed to tell anyone that he consulted no oracle.

Ogadi did nothing for a living except to drink palm wine. From season to season, and from day to day, Ogadi found solace and companionship in palm wine. At Akunne's palm wine bar he met some soul mates. Asia turned the bread winner of the family. Most times, Ogadi stole her wife's money to buy palm wine, his addiction.

CHAPTER THREE

For well over four years Ogadi abandoned the farm, Asia with the assistance of Ajulu made nail biting efforts to cater for the family.

Ogadi did not do any other work to support his family. His face turned red each time he considered his food served late; inadequate or the soup not rich enough.

"Why is the soup filled with mushroom? Is bush meat or fish not sold in the market anymore?" Ogadi has shouted on top of his voice having served his super.

Instantly, Ajulu who served the food went cold. She was shocked at his father's unkind words. Ajulu wondered why a father who failed to provide for his family should not thank goodness for being provided for. She became resentful of his father and walked away moody.

The following evening Ogadi had left the house. Ajulu, sixteen plus, went to her mother with some questions in her mouth.

"Mother, something is bothering me," Ajulu said.

"What is the matter my daughter?" Asia replied.

"I want to know whether it's the duty of a wife to provide food for her husband and children. I mean is it normal for a wife to fend for her family? I ask this question because father appears not to care about how and where we get the food we eat in this family talk less of buying clothes for us. I can tell that he doesn't support us no matter how little. I tell you mother, if that is the case, I'm afraid I wouldn't like to marry because I don't want to slave for any man in the name of husband who would always show gratitude by battering me anytime he is upset with something. By the way, why is the society designed to render women voiceless?"

"No, no, no! It's not so my daughter. I tell you truly real men make serious efforts to provide for their families. Yes, they work hard to ensure their welfare. However, wives are there as their husbands' helpers. A wife is always amiable to supporting her husband in providing for the family. Any married man worth his salt doesn't sit idly by and watch his wife assume the role of a major provider for the family. No! It'd an aberration."

"Then why is father comfortable being fed by you for many years without batting an eye lib. By so doing is it wrong to say he's a bad example? Is it not shameful?"

"Well! His own case appears different. Your father claimed the oracle banned him from farming. He doesn't want to attract the wraths of the gods to himself or family by disobeying them."

"Mother! So you believed that story that is only good for the birds. Did anybody asked him why the same oracle did not ban him from eating or is it not said that anyone who refuses to work should not eat? Father's conduct is unacceptable. I'm ashamed of him."

"My daughter, who am I to question the will of the gods. In any case, is it not better to have him as an indolent husband and father than to be widow and fatherless. I was not born yesterday. I know the pains of widowhood in this community. I tell you, widows and fatherless children are constantly taken through hell in our society."

"Mother, I tell you, your argument is neither here nor there. Anyway, I don't believe in that nonsense oracle theory. It's a product of lazy minds. My father….My father…." Ajulu said and wanted to continue when she heard her father humming.

"Eeeh! Eeeh! What did your father do?" Ogadi cut them short as he opened the door. "Oooh! I can tell mother and daughter are gossiping with me at this unholy hour. Idle minds! Useless people! Aren't you supposed to be in bed? Why do you look at me like nobody? Will you serve my food and get out of my sight before I main somebody!"

At Akunne's bar the following day, a confused Ogadi grieved over Akunne's refusal to grant him further credit. Akunne had told Ogadi point black that she was no longer available to giving him further credit noting that were there another customer hugely indebted to her as he, her business would been grounded . All appeal by Ogadi that Akume changed her position fell on deaf ear.

With friends offering Ogadi too little palm wine to drink, he was kept miserable all day. With Akunne and bar mates turning against him; and Asia removing her purse from where he usually helped himself with money from time to time, Ogadi wondered why the world had conspired against him.

For the first time in a long while Ogadi retired home early in the evening. He mourned over his fate and visited his anger on everyone at home.

"My husband, I hope all is well. You came home too early today. I hope you're enjoying good health! "Asia asked incurring her husband's wrath.

"Must I be ill before I could come back to my own house? What nonsense! Oooh, you wish me ill health? I reject it. It's because you that don't wish me well which is why mother luck rarely shines on me. Bad woman!"

"I'm sorry my husband. I didn't mean to hurt

you. It's just that you're hardly at home at this time."

"Be sorry for yourself! For goodness sake, can't I have peace in my house?" Taking a long pause Ogadi let out. "Ooh Akunne! If not that you sell the best palm wine in Akado, I'd have heaped deadly curses on you for causing me pain. All the same, may you've nightmare until you give me unlimited credit in your bar.

Five days on, Ezeife, a lazy easy going Ogadi's bar mate came calling. He had wondered why Ogadi had not been able to raise money, off set his debt and returned to the palm wine bar.

Trialing Ajulu with his eyes, Ezeife marvelled at her breathe-taking beauty. He wished he was a man of means. He would have considered marring his friend's daughter as third wife. He began to make cold calculation to achieve his wish.

"Where went you in the past five days? Why have you not been at the palm wine joint? I tell you Ogadi, you're sorely missed," Ezeife told ogadi.

"My brother, the pocket is very. It's the ravaging harmattan that has dried up everything. It's disheartening that it's now that palm wine taste is at its best that I found myself in this mess. To make the matter worse, my wicked wife appears to tie her purse round her waist, and round the cock," Ogadi lamented.

"How could a woman you married with your hard earned morning behave so badly and you fold your hands and watch her helplessly. By the way who owes her and who owes her miserable purse?

Aren't they all your property? By the way, what is the world turning to? Nonsense! Is it not her ill luck that caused you series of misfortune to the extent that the gods banned you from farming? If I were you I'd teach her a lesson in pain," Ezeife raved. "Oh – h0! You don't know my wife. She is a very bad woman. In anycase, I'll deal with her ruthlessly and in manner she would advice herself to pack out of my house for good. Just wait and see. My mind is made up. Besides, I can still marry as many women as I wish or can't?" Ogadi asked.

"Why not if not? Well let's leave talk about women so that it doesn't spoil our day. They are bad. Even my own wives are useless. Infact, they are worse than useless. My first wife is a night mare and my second is a demon. My second wife fine it difficult to cook for me especially on Afor market days. But trust me; I'm beginning to deal with her ruthlessly. In no distant future I know she would crack and cave in," Ezeife, a man known to freeze at the sight of his man-mountain husband-beater wife boasted.

"But why would women choose to have a death grip on their husbands. Ezeife, do you realize that all of us at the bar have similar bitter experience with our wives?"

"Yes Ooh! It has always been lamentations each time we discuss our wives."

With the assurance that he would pick his bill at Akunne's palm wine bar on that fateful day, elated

Ogadi followed Ezeife to the bar. Ezeife assured his friend that despite his challenge all would soon be well. He appealed to him not to abandon him then.

"How do you mean?" Ogadi asked.

"I can see that your daughter, Ajulu has grown into a beautiful young woman and ripe for marriage. So, very soon it's expected that tens of suitors would beseech your house to ask for hers of hands in marriage. I'll advise you to select for her the richest among them. You must choose for your daughter a man who can solve all your problems. You must settle for a son-in-law who could and would build you a modern house; change your ward-robe; buy you a new bicycle, and on monthly basis spoil you with money and gin." Ezeife remarked.

"Yes oooh! My brother, you've made good points. Believe you me, I never thought along this line."

"Only good points? Are you blind not to see or deaf not to hear that Uka, Okolie and Ani's houses were built for them by their sons-in-law? Even I understand that they gave it to them as condition before consenting to give their daughters to them in marriage. I pray you remember me when your time comes. I wish I'm lucky to have a daughter. My use-less wives gave me eleven sons as if I'm raising an army or a football team. Now, I'm losing out from largess's by son-in-law".

"Ooh dear! Not to worry. In your next world, you'll beget eleven daughters and eleven sons."

"Amen! My brother. You've made my day."

Following the discussion he had with Ezeife, Ogadi began to keep hope alive. He believed Ezeife who said that Ajulu's beauty would attract many rich suitors. He began to make a mental design of the mansion his would be son-in-law would build for him and made a long list of items he must buy in order to qualify to marry Ajulu. Withall the items in his possession in future, Ogadi believed he would be on top of the world. When that time comes, he knew many would bow before him. He promised himself to shame his enemies. He would ensure he closed those large mouthed bar mates out of the joint as he would buy all the Palm wine bar has in stock daily.

Ogadi resolved to start showing immense love to Ajulu, his daughter and potential cash cow. He was beclouded by his cold calculation. Ajulu tried but could not understand why her father suddenly became friendly with her.

The house vibrated at first cock-crow that early morning when Ogadi screamed in his dream in wild jubilation for getting all he ever wished for from his son-in- law. He saw himself colourfully dressed in white traditional attire with red cap to match alighting from a brand new bicycle about to begin the house warming ceremony of the beautiful mansion Ajulu's husband built for him. Ogadi lavishly entertained his guests that friends and relations stood in awe for him. Ogadi was seen as demi god by his people. He thanked mother luck for blessing him with a super rich son-in-law who always filled his pocket with cripse money notes.

Ogadi's euphoria evaporated when he suddenly woke up to realize it was all a dream. He was sad that despite the oodles of money at his disposal a few moments ago in the dream world, the discomfort he bore as a result of his inability to buy shaving stick to shave his overgrown bear worsened. He prayed God to bring his dream to realty.

CHAPTER FOUR

Ogadi took ill one evening to the absolute discomfort of the family, friend and relations. He came back Akunne's palm wine bar feeling weak and exhausted. Holding his stomach tight Ogadi began to vomit uncontrollably.

Asia and Ajulu turned emergency medics. While Asia pressed her husband's head with hot water, Ajulu cleared the mess on the floor. Asia became scared to death when Ogadi began to vomit blood. She raised the alarm. In Akado 'Community spirit' neighbour responded in a flash. While some stood watching Ogadi with helplessness written across their faces, a few were quick to profer solution to Ogadi's Condition.

"Go......Go......quickly and get garlic and palm oil. It's clear to the blind that your husband has been poisoned. It'll not be well with the evil – doer," Okafor said more or less shouting at Asia.

"There is ….. There is no garlic in the house," Asia replied nervously.

"Then quickly get coconut. We need its water. It's an antidote to poison."

"But we don't have coconut in the house too"

"Ooh Gosh! Okay, hurry get me some honey. We'll make do with it. Honey is as good as coconut water."

"We don't have honey either".

"Aaah! Do you've anything at all in this house? Your husband is dying and you stand idly by telling me you don't have this and you don't have that. What arrant nonsense!" Okafor charged and dashed out to get coconut in his house.

Moment later coconut water and palm oil were forced down Ogadi's throat. With no noticeable improvement in his condition, Ogadi was rushed to a hospital in the neighbouring village of Isiuzo.

The seventy two years old medical doctor who lived in the hospital's premises was right on hand to attend to Ogadi. He gave him some injections and placed him on a drip. He used his hands and stethoscope to examine Ogadi. Dr Uzoka was reasonably sure Ogadi has a damaged liver and acute heart problem. Also, the sick man had acute low blood level.

Dr Uzoka told Asia and others that Ogadi needed three pints of blood to buoy his blood level regretted that the hospital had no blood bank. He said that anyone with the same blood group as Ogadi could have donated some blood to save Ogadi's life but regretting the hospital had no screening machine to ascertain the suitability of such blood. He advised them to hurriedly go to a particular hospital at Idu to buy blood. Dr Uzoka drew Ogadi's blood sample and gave it to Asia to take to Idu. The doctor advisedly warned that the blood transfusion must be done in twenty four hours.

Ifeadi insisted that he donates blood to Ogadi. He assured the doctor that being first cousins he was sure there blood group would be the same. He stated that it was needless going to Idu. Besides, the money was not there for the purchase of any blood. Dr Uzoka flatly turned down Ifeadi's plea once again citing lack of blood screening machine as his reason.

Asia in her poor state could not cough out any money to buy blood for her dyeing husband. She turned to her husband's relations for help but no one offered any tangible assistance.

Many did not show any concern about Ogadi worsening health condition. Someone jokingly advised that palm wine from Akunne's palm wine bar could be used as blood for Ogadi.

Two days on, Asia could only raise money for one pint of blood. Some people joined her to go buy one pint of blood believing that could prolong

Ogadi's life while efforts would be intensified to buy the balance two pints blood.

Moment before Asia got to the hospital with one pint of blood Ogadi had passed on. Hours before he gave up the ghost, Dr Uzoka had watched helplessly as Ogadi's organs packed up one after the other.

Asia and her children wept uncontrollably. She wondered why Ogadi who was not sick prior to his going out on that evil day suddenly came back vomiting blood. Like Okafor, she suspected foul play in her husband's death. As far as she was concerned, enemies had dealt him a deadly blow. While some blamed Ogadi's death on witch craft, a voiceless few felt that Ogadi has long poisoned himself with indolence and alcohol.

Following Ogadi's extend family's emergency meeting, a decision was reached to bury Ogadi same day. Okonkwo, a cut and nail carpenter was contracted to make a coffin. Two hours later, Okonkwo delivered a coffin with embarrassing rough finishing Bathed and wrapped in length of white cloth, Ogadi was buried by his kinsmen low-key and unsung. They put on hold the performance of elaborate rites of passage for Ogadi pending when his children could do so in future.

Few days after Ogadi's internment, sympathizers dried up in Asia's house except for a few men who had some other ulterior motives. Like an abandoned ship Asia became alone. In her condition, Asia would not forget in a hurry her aunt's uncharitable remarks about Ogadi days after his death.

"Why are you crying your eyes out over the death of a never-do-well husband of yours? Why do you want to kill yourself over the demise of a loafer, indolent, lazy and drunkard husband who preferred to pass this world as a shadow instead of stamping his foot prints on the sand of time? Why are you weeping over the inglorious passage of a husband who failed to support his family but rather choose to blame his failure on the gods? Asia, don't you know that all that oracle theory was an organized deception?" Aunty Bridget enquired with the eye of an angry man. She paused for lengthy moments and took a deep breath. Not done yet she locked her eyes fiercely into Asia's and continued.

"My daughter, if the truth must be told, every-one knows you've been a widow for donkey years. Rather than weep over the death of a husband that was never indeed a husband you ought to be cursing the day you married him. Long before his death, Ogadi had been a living dead and a nightmare. My daughter, pray that in your next world your paths would not cross. Wipe your tears and be hopeful. One day, some day, men that deserve you will …eeh….eeh….you know come to your aid. You're a beautiful woman."

Asia was not in the least comfortable with Bridget's sweeping remarks about her late husband even though they were not far from the truth. She felt that no matter what custom and decency do not permit anyone to talk ill of the dead, Ogadi inclusive. Asia recalled within herself that Ogadi was a tall, athletic built and the most handsome suitor asking her hand in marriage. That was way back in time. As a teenager she considered her acceptance of Ogadi's hands in marriage as the best decision she ever made in life. That things turned out ugly were well outside her control.

Overwhelmed by emotion, tears pool in her eyes but Asia could not release them for fear Aunty Bridget's wrath. Meanwhile, Ajulu who eavesdropped in the discussion from her room agreed absolutely, though sadly, with Aunty Bridget's views about her late father. It confirmed her belief that her father was a let down and a bad example to fatherhood. Ajulu recalled in deep pain that many a time she and her siblings went to bed on empty stomach all because their father refused to embrace hard work and choose to be married to palm wine.

CHAPTER FIVE

Ajulu got married to Obi, a tall, dark complexed and handsome young man in his early thirties. Obi was the only son of Maduka, a famous farmer in the neighbouring village of Ani-Ugo. Obi was the last among Maduka's five children.

Obi's mother Adaeke, a woman known for her arrogance and hot temper, was believed to have an over-bearing influence on her husband and children. Her word was law in the household and many avoid attracting her wrath to themselves. Whenever she is annoyed, the fury of hell was a child's play.

The marriage ceremony between Ajulu and Obi was elaborate with all expenses gladly picked by Maduka. The renowned farmer's family was happy when obi that had shied away from marrying despite the pressure brought to bear on him for many years came back; one fateful evening to gladly announce that he was ready to marry. The news was received and celebrated by Maduka's household. The need to grow the family tree was urgent and uppermost in their mind.

Adaeke, with a sense of urgency, went to town employing her social network to find a suitable wife for her son, Obi. In no time, about twenty one spinsters were recommended and contacted in Ani-Ugo but none of them met the desired qualities Adaeke wanted in a would-be daughter-in-law.

After each 'Screening' session, Adaeke would tell the girl sometimes before her point blank that she is not good enough for her beloved Son, Obi. A few were saddened by her posture. Adaeke found fault with each and every one of them. She would complain about the girl's complexion, height, dentition and all what not. On one occasion Adaeke rejected her bosom friend's daughter on ground of being a candidate for obesity. She attracted her friend's wrath.

"My good friend, I'm shocked to my marrow that you could use derogatory words on my daughter's physique. In any case, your indolent son, a product of voodoo, who refused to do anything for a living is equally not good for my daughter. Tell him to be man enough to go look for a wife for himself. Tell him that if he must marry, he should embrace hard work so as to support his family. Tell him to grow up."

"Eliza, did I hear you right? I mean, you had the guts to call my beloved son, obi names? You called him a product of voodoo all because I rejected your wayward daughter as my would-be daughter-in-law. You'll pay for this I promise you."

"Pay for what? I ask, pay for what? I'll repeat it a thousand times and in any forum that your irresponsible son, Obi, is a product of voodoo. Don't forget so soon that hand in hand we worked tirelessly to make it happen. And instead of showing some appreciation, here you're castigating ny beloved daughter, Chinelo."

"Well! I think you've jealous and bitter. I don't want to waste my precious time with a bitch who can't manage her home. Anyway, you've always been a bad news"

"Ooh Adaeke! You're the temerity to insult me? A woman who though in her husband's house is 'married' to several men out there. Is it not about time you confess your adulterous life? Do I need to remind you that desperate effort to beget a male child before you resorted to voodoo? Shameless woman!" Eliza terribly disappointed thundered.

Undetened, Adaeke who was determined not to settle for second best as wife for obi with missionary zeal extended her search net to neighbouring communities which caught Ajulu.

As soon as Ajulu arrived Maduka's house, Adaeke barred her from doing any household chores. According to Obi's mother all she wanted Ajulu to do was to bear her grand children. "All I want from you is to bear ten children for me --- six boys and four girls."

Obi was seldom at home. He went visiting friends in and around Ani-Ugo. Ajulu wondered why her husband would not go work with his father on the farm. She prayed that the spirit of Ogadi had not reincarnated in Obi. Many a time he complained to Adaeke about Obi's conducts she was always quick to advice Ajulu to be patient with Obi as he had been an out – going person. On one occasion Adaeke told Ajulu to leave Obi alone wondering whether she was not well fed.

Seven months into Ajulu's marriage, an impatient Adaeke summoned Ajulu to her room at noon. Scanning her body fiercely with her eyes, Adaeke enquired.

"I don't seem to be seeing any changes in your body. It has become a matter of deepest concern to me and the family. What is actually going on? Have you forgotten that this family has no time to waste?"

"Mother! I don't understand, "Ajulu who appeared to be caught off guard replied with her heart pounding hard on the chest.

"Ooh! You claim not to understand me, right? All well and good! To put it plainly, I want to know whether you're pregnant. For obvious reasons, it's of grave concern to me."

"Mother, I don't know".

"You don't know whether you're pregnant?

This is funny. I can tell you're a bare-faced lier. I didn't know I married a toddler for my loved son. But you'd better grow up" Adaeke yelled boiling on the inside.

Three years on, the hostility on Ajulu who had several miscarriages, by Adaeke and her children became unbearable. Adaeke began to hate Ajulu with passion. Her presence irritated her mother-in-law. Thought of Ajulu killed Adaeke's appetite. She instigated her children to mock and insult Ajulu. Day by day, the bruise Ajulu's psyche by making derogatory remarks at her. They call her a man and labelled her a witch.

Ajulu swam in emotional trauma. Maduka's cautioning voice was drowned. He could not stand firm as age was telling on him. Obi stood aloof. He appeared unbothered by his wife's plight. It seems hell crashed on Ajulu's feet and she had no hiding place.

Five years on, with the frustration arising from Ajulu's in ability to bear a child at its highest pitch, an emergency family meeting was summoned one morning by Adaeke. Maduka had gone to attend a village meeting. Red face on the face, Adaeke told the meeting comprising her sister and children that the agenda of the meeting was to discuss Ajulu's childlessness, its implication for the family and the way forward.

"Let's start by asking Ajulu or whatever she is called why she refused to give us a child in this family or has she used her womb for other things. I mean witchcraft precisely. I understand that her people are neck deep into voodoo. Also, I was her reliably informed that many young women in her community sacrifice their womb to the marine spirit for power and beauty," Adaeke who sounded like the complainant, prosecutor and judge in her matter set the floor rolling.

"With due respect mother I don't know all what you're talking about. However, I'm faithful that God will give me a child at his own time," Ajulu writhing in pain replied. "Now tell me, do you belong to the marine world? I mean do you have a marine husband?" Theresa, Adaeke's elder sister asked full of hatred and resentment of Ajulu.

"Aunty, with due respect, I don't know what you're talking about. And I take exception to that demeaning question."

"You're a bloody liar. Looking at your eyes I'm dead sure you've been positioned by the evil one to wreak havoc in this family but make no mistake, you and your sponsors will fail. Also, take it from me that your witchcraft will kill you. I regret marrying you for my beloved son, obi. Truly appearance can be deceptive," Adaeke said with venom in her voice.

The following day, Ajulu, a breathe away from self explosion went to see her mother in Akado. Absolutely disheartened and in hot tears, she told Asia all what happened. Ajulu told her mother that all things considered she had decided to quit her marriage for good. She added that she was on the brink of losing her insanity. To Ajulu, she could not stand being labelled a witch and a mermaid spirit.

Asia, a lesson in patience, consoled her. She advised her to exercise extreme patience in her situation as that was the only effective medicine to cure marital challenges. She told Ajulu to remember the story of the proverbial bed bug that advised her children to be patient as whatever was hot will be cool. Asia told her daughter to be hopeful of better days ahead as to live is to hope.

Asia told her daughter that it was a well known fact that she conceived and bore her first child in her eight year of marriage. Asia confessed that could account partly as to why her husband, Ogadi, in the zenith of frustration found solace in alcohol.

CHAPTER SIX

Ajulu became Maduka's family's night mare following her inability to give them a child. Their frustration filled the cup and was over flowing. She was treated with leprosy hatred and a few wanted her head on the axe.

Seven years counted, another family meeting was held that excluded Ajulu. Adaeke and Obi's eldest sister Ngozi without mincing words told Obi to consider seriously marrying another wife and raising children for the family. They told him point blank that Ajulu was positioned by the forces of darkness to shot down Maduka's family. Adaeke added that, that was the finding of some spiritualists.

Smiling from cheek to cheek, Obi thanked members' of his family for their deep concern and understanding of his unfortunate condition. He told them bluntly that there was nothing to consider as he had taken proactive action on the matter.

"One of my concubines had given me a child and as a matter-of-fact would be delivered of a second one any time soon."

Jumping to her feet, Adaeke screamed in ecstasy.

"Holy God! That is a smart move by you my beloved so. No matter what the world thinks, I've always known that you're as wise as King Solomon. But why did your hide this joyous news from us all this while? Anyway, this is the greatest and sweetest news of the moment. It calls for celebration and we must celebrate it right away."

"'I'm sorry mother that I kept the whole thing to myself. It's just that I don't know how Ajulu, a wife you chose for me would feel"

"Which Ajulu? I ask which Ajulu. You mean a woman that refused to give us a child because of her evil motive? What nonsense! As far as I'm concerned, she is a non-issue. Her feeling does not matter anymore not in the least. When she had made this family a laughing stock in this community. Thank goodness you've been vindicated at last. The fault isn't yours my son. Ajulu is bad news and worse than bad news. Now, I hate her with passion to the extent that I'm irritated by the way she talks, walks, laughs and even by her presence."

Ngozi, an extrovert, who claimed to be a 'convert', was quick to raise some praise and worship songs. In a flash, everyone joined her to mouth the chorus.

As members of Maduka's family sang and danced in celebration of the fruit of Obi's extra-marital activity, Ajulu who was washing clothes about ten metres away wondered why the Maduka were in joyous mood. Being a stanger in her husband's house, she hoped that sooner than later she would know the facts behind all that was happening.

The entrance of Maduka into the house brought the meeting abruptly to an end. The octogenarian lost a heat beat. Looking confused at what was happening, the frail-looking old man was transfixed like a statue for a short while.

"What is going on here?" Maduka asked no one in particular gazing in wonder.

"Nothing serious my husband. It's just that we decided to have a short family prayer meeting. We want to thank God for his love, mercy, guardians and protection; and make our supplications to him. Also, through prayer we cast out and bind all demonic forces operating in this family. Time has come to wage spiritual war against them," Adaeke said smiling warmly. Many believed she had a tight grip on her husband. Adaeke appeared to call the shots.

Maduka knew that his wife was not telling the whole story. Before he could make further remarks everyone had melted away from the living room, venue of the 'prayer meeting'.

Adaeke was sad that she failed to enquire about that sex of her grand child. Adaeke was however confident that Ajulu would sooner that later be taken out of the family's equation should she remain childless.

Hours later, Adaeke took Obi to her room to enable her ask him the most important question of the moment.

"A girl child!" Adaeke exclaimed, narrowing her eye brow and tightening her face. Even the blind could see she was not vey happy.

"Not to worry mother! I believe the child about to be born would be a male child. Trust me." Obi said.

"We must make effort to bring mother and child into this family. This is their house."

Obi never liked the idea of having two wives under his roof. He believed one wife was more than enough challenge for any man. His uncle's bitter experience was a good lesson for any young man habouring the idea of marrying two or more wives under the same roof. It had been fierce's throat. Driven by jealousy and intolerance, the warring wives sometimes engaged in physical combat and went diabolical to undo each other in effort to gain upper hand in attracting their husband's love and attention. No week rolled by without a major crisis in Oke's house that would call for neighbours intervention.

Oke, husband of three wives and twenty one children grief and watch helplessly while his house was continually on fire. To people's disbelief, he always appeared subdued and conquered. Before long, he became anabsentee husband and father. To him, he was living in hell.

Obi was determined to avoid Oke's mistakes all cost despite the pressure on him by Adaeke to bring his concubine and child into the house. Unknown to obi, his mother had started visiting comfort and child secretly. She was bringing pressure to bear on them to move into Maduka's house assuring that they would be welcomed and catered for.

CHAPTER SEVEN

As Comfort's expected date of delivery drew near, she yielded to Adaeke's pressure to move into Obi's father's house.One morning, precisely at 5.30am, Comfort with her two year old child strapped to her back stood fidgety in Muduka's entrance door. A frighetened Comfort, a victim of low self esteem could not summon the courage to rap on the door. Many a time she raised her hand to knock but she brought it down in panick. She was not sure how Maduka's family would react to her action.

Cough by her daughter which tended to give her away panicked her into action. Adaeke made for the door. On hearing a gentle tap on the door. Without enquiring who the visitor was, she opened the door. Beaming with smile, Adaeke warmly welcomed Comfort and her grand child.

"Ewwoo! Ewwooo! Come in my daughter! Come in my daughter. What a pleasant surprise!" Adaeke said swimming in Joy unspeakable. "Maduka, Obi, Ngozi, Ify....... Where are you? Come quickly and see what the lord has done!"

In no time, everyone assembled at the palour. A visibly angry Obi could not believe his eyes. He was rudely shocked and embrarrased by Comfort's presence. He recalled that he warned comfort time without number never to come close to his family house until he deemed it appropriate. He wondered why a mere concubine would flout his order. He was at a loss as to what was her motive. Locking his eyes fiercely into Comfort's eyes for a brief moment, Comfort's heart pounded heavily on her chest.

"What are you doing here? I ask, what are you doing here? Didn't I warn you never and to ......"Obi said but was cut short by his mother.

"Never to do what? I ask never to do what? What nonsense! Is this child not yours? Does the pregnancy not belong to you? Whether anybody likes it or not, they are in their home and they have come to stay for good. Our difference in this matter is irreconcilable."

Maduka looked on in disbelief as his wife tackled Obi. His mouth went dry.

Ajulu was transfixed with tears of betrayal forming in his eyes. She was profoundly disappointed at her husband, Obi.

"Obi, why did you do this to me? What did I do to deserve this cruel treatment? Why... why.."

Ajulu lamented attracting Adaeke's wrath.

"Why did my son do to you? What cruel treatment are you talking about? Look at you, a woman who carried a can of shame on her head having the guts to complain. You've crossed the line and you've me to contend." Adaeke replied feigning deep anger. "Let me remind you that you failed woefully to give me grand children. The beautiful woman here has made me proud. She has given me a grand child and another is on the way. This is no mean feat. And here you're shedding crocodile tears. In you, the devil is a liar. I warn you, your treatment of this matter would spell joy and sadness, life or death for you in this house. One person can't embrace the iroko tree."

Maduka drew Obi close and whispered something into his ears, and left the sitting room. Ajulu feeling like a worthless piece of rag went into her room weeping openly. Adaeke's hate-filled face hunted her. Ajulu's cry aroused Obi's emotion. He was moved to pity.

"Comfort, Comfort, Comfort!" Obi called visibly angry. "I can tell you want to break my marriage. I warn you, go back to where you came from. Do just that right away. Don't test my will. Don't dare me because you'll live to regret it."

"Which marriage does she want to break? Do you really have a marriage? Do you mean this sham of a marriage that could not give me grand children? As things stand now, let the sky fall, Comfort my daughter is going no where. For goodness sake, we can't be in abundance of water and yet thirst. The family must not go into oblivion. The love portion that evil woman, Ajulu, fed you has been rendered ineffective from today. You had better stop fighting, a lost battle. Stop living a lie," Adaeke screeched, adjusting her wrapper as if she poised for a fight. She stamped her feet on the floor continually.

Ajulu, though feeling unloved did not deem it necessary to take her burden to her mother anymore because she knew that Asia in her characteristic manner would advise her to be patient. Ajulu saw Comfort's instruction into her matrimony as one of the many crosses fate bestowed on her. She made up her mind to bear it without drawing rain. Against all expectation she refused to discuss Comfort matter with anyone. It died on her heart, painfully though.

Ajulu's comportment panicked every one in the family. She pretended all was well and went about her business. Adaeke was inwardly disturbed. She wondered what was in Ajulu's mind. She wishes Ajulu said something about the development in the family.

CHAPTER EIGHT

Everyone was surprised to note that Obi who had refused to answer Comfort's greeting for weeks started spending quality time with her in her room. Unknown to many Comfort's miem had always warmed her into Obi's heart. This development threw Ajulu into deeper grief she had hoped that Comfort would be frustrated out of the house should Obi give her cold shoulders for long. Ajulu wondered why Comfort went through the process of rejection, accommodation and acceptance by Obi while hers was the reverse.

Ajulu felt she was losing Obi's attention by the day. She regretted that age and ill health appear to be rendering the patriarch of the family, Maduka invalid otherwise he was the only person she could turn to. Even the toddler knew that Maduka's views on family matters were being ignored.

Ajulu in her pain heaped the blame of her marital crisis on her mother-in-law. She cursed the day Adaeke stepped into her father's house with a local wax wrapper as gift to woo her into marrying her son, Obi.

Forty-five days later, Comfort was delivered of a baby girl. Adaeke was saddened beyond description when the news about the arrival of the baby was given to her. She managed to give a weak smile. She desperately wanted a male child. From that moment her relationship with Comfort became lukewarm and later nose-dived. Adaeke ensured that no naming ceremony took place contrary to her earlier plan. Also, the planned formalization of the marriage between Comfort and Obi was suspended indefinitely by Adaeke. She was considering looking for yet another woman for Obi who could bear a male child for the family in the event of Comfort not bearing a boy child.

Noticing the warning attention being given to her, Comfort began to bring out her true colour. She became quarrelsome and nagged at practically everyone. Comfort exchanged hot words with anyone who dared to oppose her view in any matter. In no time, she turned abusive. She was quick to heap curse on Obi for not taking good care of her as promised. Comfort accused Obi of crass deception and bringing her life to ruin. She told whoever cares to listen that Obi had consistently maintained he was single but changed his story line when he had put her in family way. Obi confessed that he had a wife who was forced on him by his 'over bearing' mother.

Obi, according to Comfort said he did not love Ajulu and their marriage was as good as over. Obi encouraged her to commence elaborate plan for their grand marriage ceremony; on that would be the talk – of – town for decades.

It was in the process of putting finishing touches to the marriage plan that Comfort discovered that she was carrying another baby for Obi. Obi was quick to remind her that going by custom and tradition he could not pay her bride price in her condition.

Meanwhile, Obi was a happy man. Though it had become a season of lies by him, he was able to confirm that Ajulu's inability to conceive and bear children was squarely her fault. He freed himself from psychological trauma. Obi walked with his head high.

Adaeke held Ajulu responsible for Comfort's bad manners.She reasoned that if Ajulu who came into the family and enjoyed tones of love and goodwill did not squander them by not bearing a child; Comfort would not have come into the picture. For every bit of insult on her by Comfort, Ajulu bore the brunt. Adaeke made life unbearable for Ajulu. In all this, Obi stayed aloof.

With the death of Maduk, Adaeke after the mourning period became determined to bring everyone in Maduka's family under her firm control. However, Adaeke's desire that her words would be laws was resisted by her children. A few of them had been sick and tired of her high-handedness and over bearing influence on the family. This gave her nightmares.

In six years, Comfort had four children, all girls and two miscarriages. The medical doctor at the health centre advisedly warned her to stop child bearing due to her debilitating hypertension but Adaeke in desperate quest for a male child would not hear of it. Adaeke, Seventy five, had practically gone biserk over the male child challenge in the family. She continued to vent her anger on Ajulu, a woman, she believed brought ill-luck to her family.

One fateful day, Adaeke rained curses on Ajulu all day. For daring to stop her mother-in-law from heaping abuses at her, Ajulu attracted Obi's wrath. She got a black eye for it.

"Who are you talking back at? My mother! Ooh! She has become your mate ear!"

"Didn't you hear her rain deadly curses at me? What did I do to warrant this hatred and mistreatment by her? Is it my fault that I did not bear you a child?"

"Shut your stinking mouth. Whose fault is it? Certainly it's not my fault. You idiot! The next time you exchange words with my mother I'll cut off your tongue, Obi thundered.

"But why did you fail to caution your mother? Why is she wicked and hateful of me? Why is she this evil?" Ajulu blurted.

"My mother is what? Did I hear you right? Did you say my mother is wicked and evil?"

Before Ajulu could respond, Obi descended on her. On the floor and writhing in pain hold of Obi's leg.

"Kill me ooo! Obi, you must kill me today!" She cried aloud.

Inwardly, Adaeke was happy Obi had taught Ajulu a lesson in pain. Adaeke knew she had a son who could protect her. She felt real good.

CHAPTER NINE

Maduka's family was thrown into deep mourning when Comfort died during child bearing. The medical doctor who had battled to save Comfort's life wished Comfort heeded his warning on the danger of carrying another pregnancy following her debilitating high blood pressure and acute diabetics.

Tongues continued to wag as to who killed Comfort. Expectedly, Adaeke was quick to point accusing finger at Ajulu. Though financially distressed, she borrowed money at a cut throat interest to buy required drinks which she reported the matter to Ndidibie (a group of native and witch doctors).

Ajulu was compelled to swear to an oath with a white sheep to the effect that she did not have a hand directly or indirectly in the death of Comfort. As was customary, Ajulu's people were in attendance. It was believed that if Ajulu was guilty of the offense, her body would swell in three years otherwise she would be deemed innocent. And her relations, friends and well wishers were expected to dress in white attire, roll out the drums and the attention of natives that the gods had vindicated her. She could throw an elaborate party to celebrate as many had done.

Many could not figure out why Adaeke intensified the war she waged against Ajulu despite the Ndidibies' intervention in the matter. Adaeke refused food prepared by Ajulu and any form of assistance by her. Ajulu had wanted peace to reign in Maduka's house at all cost.

"Hey! Hey!! Hey!!! Take your food away, you evil woman. Or do you want to poison me, yes, do you want to kill me as you killed Comfort. If the world claims not to know who you are, I do. You're evil.Curse be the day you agreed to marry my son but greater curse meets the person who recommended you to me. Evil will never depart from his house," Adaeke cursed, hissed viciously, eying Ajulu evily.

A Few months later, with the increased challenges posed by Obi's daughters and the clear reluntance of his sisters to help out, Obi's turned to Ajulu for assistance. A willing Ajulu met stiff resistance in the fast ageing Adaeke.

"Hey! Hey!! Hey!!! Don't ever touch my grand children with your your evil hand. Or do..... do..... you want to.... to......" Adaeke yelled at Ajulu on the occasion she was giving Chika a bathe. But she was cut short by Obi.

"Mother! Mother!! Enough of this harassment of my beloved wife, Ajulu. What has she done to warrant all this. Why do you habour morbid hatred for her. Why do you want fromher. Why do you traumatize her? For goodness sake, let her be. I'm sick and tired of your maltreatment of Ajulu." Obi charged at her mother.

How dare you talk to melike that?Me your mother, symbol and matriarch of the family? Oh! Ajulu has become your beloved wife? You've become blind to her evil. Let me remind you that Ajulu's motive is to close this family but she wouldn't succeed as long as I live."

"Ah mother! How could you say a thing like that? You know it's not true! I know that somewhere down road of life, Ajulu will be vindicated."

"I can tell Ajulu, a woman I regretted marrying for you with my hard earned money have bewitched you. You can't think straight anymore!" Adaeke said breathing heavily. "All right, be reminded that first, Ajulu tied her womb and refused to give you a child. Second, she caused Comfort not to give you a male child through witchcraft manipulation, and third, she killed mother and child in the labour room. Didn't the dockita (doctor) say Comfort was being delivered of a male child when she died? I can go on and on to reel out Ajulu's evil activities. Make no mistake, in three years Ajulu would pay the steep price of her evil. Nemesis is about to catch up with her. Ajulu will confess to her evil deeds. Thereafter, she will die a miserable death."

Ajulu stood helplessly and sobbed as her mother-in-law heaped wicked allegations on her. She prayed God of Justice to vindicate her.

Obi, though, distressed began to develop soft spot for his persecuted wife, Ajulu. With little money in his pocket, Obi who did nothing for living took solace in drinking local gin. Many wondered why he gulped a glass of a gin at a go. In no time, even the blind could see the adverse impact of gin on Obi's physique. Dry like a stock fish, Obi more often than not was brought back home by Good Samaritans, sometimes in a wheel barrow.

Obi was nicknamed Baba Gin or BG for short by some youths, some young enough to be his sons. He was happy at whoever hailed him with his hands waving at the person. Obi's nuisance value in Ani-Ugo worsens by the day. Ajulu was saddened by her husband's conduct. She saw her late father Ogadi, re-incarnate in Obi.

Obi's sisters were continually embarrassed by his drunkenness. Adaeke got depressed by the moment. She was at a loss as to why fate was unkind to her.

CHAPTER TEN

Obi woke up one morning and announced to his family that he was leaving for the city in search of white collar job to enable him support the family. He said he would no longer stay in a community that perceived him as a loafer and less than a man.

No one believed her ears. It was hoped that they heard him right.

Obi my beloved son, are you kidding? What is the problem? Why this sudden decision? I hope you thought through the implication of your decision," Adaeke asked looking worried.

"Yes mother, I did," replied Obi.

"Obi my son, why do you want to abandon you primary responsibility as the man of the house? Have you forgotten that we need male protection in this family? We may be finished in this community when you're gone. My son, I beg of you in the name of God and your ancestors to reconsider your decision. Please stay with us. We need you more than you can ever imagine," Adaeke pleaded with Obi on a kneeling position.

"I'm sorry mother; my mind is made up on the matter. I'm sick and tired of being mocked by natives. Besides, I don't want to be fed by you anymore," Obi said looking up-tight.

"But have you forgotten that there is compelling need for male protection in this family? To me, that ranks highest in our order of needs," Adacke insisted amidst tears. Her heart beat increased many folds.

"God will protect you all," Obi blurted.

Ajulu looked on in total disbelief. Unknown to them, a fellow native, Ibe, had tonge-lashed Obi for pouring away the only glass of local gin he could afford on that day at a particular bar. He insisted that Obi should replace the drink but he could not. Matter-of-fact, Obi was awaiting the arrival of a friend who promised to buy him drink when the incident happened.

Despite Obi's passionate appeal for forgiveness, Ibe boiling on the inside stopped short of pouncing on Obi. With eyes that turned red, Ibe rained insults on Obi. He called him unprintable names. It took the intervention of some bar mates to rescue Obi from the hands of Ibe.

Upon deep reflection, Obi noted that though in the past people had called him names but no one had been as hostile and aggressive as Ibe. On getting home, he refused to eat the dinner Ajulu served him. All through the night, Obi tossed and turned on the bed. He saw Ibe's negative remarks as a wakeup call. Since he had Phobia for farm work, he decided to go to the city in search of white collar job.

A fortnight later while Adaeke was beginning to believe that Obi had changed his mind, Obi left his land of origin for Lagos, the centre of excellence and a metropolitan city that meant different things to different people. To some, Lagos is a land of hope and opportunities. And to others, it is a land of shattered dreams, centre of crime and deception. Yet to others this land of aquatic splendour is just a victim of unrealistic expectation.

The wailing of Adaeke, Ajulu and his children failed to stop Obi from leaving Ani-Ugo. With his few cloths in the polythene bag, Obi was gone.

Obi's action was the beginning of a long nightmare for Adaeke. She felt dispised and abandoned. She bemoaned her situation and wish death should come calling. From the moment of Obi's exit, the family felt insecure and lived in fear.

After a long and strenuous search, Obi,late at night found and moved in with his seventy eight years.

Maternal uncle who lived in Amukoko; a slump in the suburb of Lagos. Adim had retired fifteen months before Obi joined him as a senior Messenger in the Ministry of Transport at an official age of sixty. He had doctored his age severally through court affidavits. Adim had always stated in the affidavits that as at the time he was born there ways no birth register in his community. The septuagenarian had a wife and nine children all living in one room in a twenty room bungalow the local folks call 'face-me-I-face-you'. One hundred and five people live in the house.

The tenants' shared two pit toilets and two bathrooms built with corrugated zinc. There were always quarrels and fights as to who would clean up the usually messed up latrine until the landlord intervened and prepared a duty roaster for the occupants of his house.Mornings were always soaked with tension as tenantsqueue to have their bathe. Anyone who spent more time then the three minutes unofficially allocated time instantly attracted the wraths of those in the queue.

Obi would not forget how a young woman, Maggie, was shouted at and almost dragged out from the bathroom stack naked for over staying her unofficially approved time. Angry words were thrown at her. Many had wondered why Maggie who was unemployed took joy in wasting other people's time who were eager to get to their work places. Many demonized her. However, she hurriedlycame out looking unperturbed.

With everyone cooking at the veranda, food stuffs and soup ingredients sometimes develop wings. Some women who were privileged to cook red meat or chicken part practically showcased them to arouse ill feeling in their fellow women.

Adim, an alcoholic and a man that had many concubines in his neighborhood had always lived from hand-to-mouth. While in service, his meager salary hardly took him to the tenth day of a new month. He was always indebted from drinking joints to food stuff sellers. So, Obi appearing unexpectedly that night with the 'bad news' that he had come to stay with his family set Adim on fire. But he could not turn Obi back. First, Obi was his nephew.Second, Adim recalled challenging Obi many a time on occasion he went to the village on annual leave to leave the village and come to enjoy city life. It was a challenge Adim in his wildest imagination never thought Obi would ever take up because of his perceived love for Ani-Uyo. Adim has always blown his status out of proportion whenever his visited the village.

All things considered, Adim with a false smile welcomed Obi to his 10"x12" room at Amukoko. Maria could not believe that her husband of thirty-three years considering their poor condition could ask his Nephew to come stay with them. Like a submissive wife she had been, Maria did not challenge her husband. However, deep down in her she saw Adim's action as the height of insensitivity to their family challenges.

Obi joined Adim's adult children many of them

without education or vocation in keeping late night outside in an environment that does not sleep. They come in, clean up and dash out. Two of Adims daughters were fond of disappearing throughout the night. In the morning, they would always claim they passed the night at one neighbour or the other's house which was convenient to the Adims. Not until Chinasia was discovered to be four months pregnant that the activities of the girls were clear to all and sundry. Unfortunately, the man Chinasia claimed was responsible for her pregnancy denied strenuously accusing Chinasia of being a whore.

Maria was hard hit by the bitter experience. She believed she had been made a laughing stock in the neighbourhood. Maria was particularly disturbed that her daughter's conduct might rode off onher negatively in the church. She had nightmares. She was further taken through hell by her husband who shifted all the blame for their daughter's crass misconduct on her.

"You see the shame you and your useless daughter have brought on this family. Because of your gross negligence, we've been made a laughing stock in this neighbourhood. Yes, because you failed in your duties as a mother I can't no longer walk with my head up in a neighbourhood I've stayed for thirty-seven years. You're a disgrace to motherhood. You failed woefully to bring up your daughter mannerly and here you've shedding crocodile tears," Adim shouted at a weeping Maria.

At the church service one fateful Sunday, the officiating priest appeared to have directed his homily at Maria. The Priest has accused parents of failing woefully in their responsibilities to their children by not teaching them morals and as a consequence millions of them end up on the street hating virtues and adoring vices.

"What do we see today?" He asked no one in particular taking a brief pause. "We see school dropouts; prostitution at its peak; teenage pregnancies; drug addiction; cultism, indolence; drunkenness 419 ritualists to mention but a few vices shaking the foundation of this generation. Money had become god. Material acquisition has become our bane. Parents have abandoned their primary responsibility of bring up their children in the fear of God in blind pursuit of money. By so doing, failed man and God. The judgment of God is awaiting each and every one of us on the last day. Brothers and sister in the Lord, we must retrace our steps now before it's too late. Because verily, verily, I tell you, hell fire is starring you right on the face."

Maria, condemned by conscience was numbed in the church she moped throughout the remaining part of the service. She went into deep thought about the characters of her children and felt that the Priest was absolutely right. She wondered who told him their family's story. She panicked at the thought of going to hell fire.

Not until the worshippers started leaving the

church in droves did Maria realized that the Mass was over. She went home consoled in the knowledge that her husband had roles to play in moulding the character of their children.

CHAPTER ELEVEN

Two years on, Obi could not find the white collar job that took him to Lagos. He had no education or trade. He did not communicate with his family nor want to go back to the village. All Ajulu heard from somebody who saw Obi in Lagos was that he was doing fine. In her characteristic manner, Ajulu saw Obi's abandonment as another cross she was fated to carry. She was determined painfully though to bear it. She hoped for better days ahead.

Meanwhile, Adim and Obi had become notorious alcoholic in the neighourhood. The duo drank alcohol like fish drank water. When asked why he was need deep into alcohol, Adim was quick to state that he used it to combat the stress the evil ones slammed on him.

One hot afternoon, Adim's nephew, Osi, a Feederal Government sponsored post graduate student in Germany stopped by to greet his uncle and family. Aside from taking Osi hours to locate Adim's house situated on an unnamed street.

Osi was appalled at the condition he met his uncle. He felt it was not even fit for domestic animals. Osi was quick to voice his feeling.

"Uncle it's nice to see you after donkey years! I had to wonder for hours before locating your house. Why are the streets not named or houses numbered? Everyone I enquired about this street end up telling me to go left and go right. In the end, it led me nowhere. Uncle, it's hell locating your house. What manner of people resides in this environment?" Osi asked.

"Well! Blame it on government who failed to develop this place. Things have been the same since I moved in thirty seven years ago. In fact, I'm the first occupant of this house. Even at that life was good in those good old days," Adim replied.

"Uncle, how do you cope with the crowd in this room? You can't continue this way. I believe time has come to figure out some better options".

"Well! Blame my situation on the government who could not provide decent and affordable accommodation for the masses. In any case, we've been managing life here all this while. Besides, we're doing better than some next door neighbours. For instance, we're only twelve in this room but the man at the extreme has seventeen people in his room."

"Do you have portable water and electricity

here?"

"Hmmm! Who dash monkey banana? We make do with hurricane lamp. But again, blame it on government who failed in her responsibility to provide social amenities to the people. We fetch coloured water from one rickety well some metres away."

"Where is Obi? I understand he lives here too. Is he gainfully employed now?"

"For where? Who dash monkey banana! He is among the millions of unemployed youth in the job market. In this country only people with high level contact get jobs. The poor is on his own. I tell you, God will judge our rulers who ought to provide jobs but failed. It's self-evident that there is a conspiracy among our rulers to improvish the masses. In this country government is heartless."

Adim was disappointed when Osi told him that he was on the verge of completing his PhD course in Civil Engineering in Frankfort, Germany. He could not understand why Osi who left the shores of the country seven year ago chose to spend all his time in the University acquiring various degrees while his people at home were wallowing in abject poverty. He saw Osi as an extremely selfish person. Adim's disappointment hit the roof top when Osi gave him a pair of black socks as gift.

Some expectant Adim's children could not believe their eyes when Osi, stood and gave each and every one of them a bear-hug with outgiving them any gift. For a relation who came from Germany, they considered Osi's action as mean. Adim's family who expected some financial assistance from Osi was literally thrown into mourning. They stopped short of cursing him.

A few months after Osi's visit, a high-powered delegation came from Ani-Ugo. They were sent by the Ani-Ugo Elders-in-Council. There mission was to bring Adim and his family back home. They were under strict instruction not to return without them.

Adim's family was thrown into confusion. Adim however recalled that thirty-two years back similar treatment was meted to Okafor, his third cousin. He knew the consequences of turning down the elders' request. It would amount to crass disobedience and the punishment is excommunication.

Unknowned to Adim, the elders decision were engineered by Osi. He had complained bitterly to his Kinsmen about the savage condition he met Adim and his family in Lagos. Osi had appealed to the elders of his community to act fast to rescue Adim who appeared unable to rescue himself from savagery.

With nine months rent in arrears and source of food becoming closed, Adim quickly took his wife and six children back to Ani-Ugo, their land of origin.

Adim's home coming was a mix bag of joy and sorrow. He was pleasantly surprised at the warm reception his people gave him. While he had two rooms in his father's mud house, another cousin and childhood friend offered him one room in this house. It was an offer Adim grabbed with a million thanks. Yet another cousin offered him a piece of land to farm. However, some mocked him openly while a few threw veiled insults on Adim's face.

"My brother Adim, you can tell that no matter how bad one's condition is, his people would always be there to rehabilitate him. The problem with you city dwellers is that you pretend a lot. You create the false impression that all is well with you when in actual fact even the blind could see you're suffering terribly. Anyway, don't give up hope on life. Be assured that here you'd not die of hunger. You can till the ground and feed your family. I offer to give you a piece of land to farm and three hundred yam seedlings. This I do free of charge," Osundu said sounding important.

Like many people in the family meeting Osundu was inwardly happy that one of the city dwellers who in the past made them look inferior had been ferried home looking helpless. Osundu could testify that Adim's weather beaten shoes which pointed skyward said it all about his condition.

Adim saw many mocking faces directed at firm. He did not to leave Lagos to avoid this sort of experience. Adim felt reduced below the stature of a man but felt he had no dignity left.

Adim's children who refused to return to the village with him were quick to go their various ways. Obi moved in with Kalu, a seventy two year old bachelor acquaintance of his. They had always met at the beer palour few houses away from Adim's former abode.

Kalu was held in awe by all. He was considered as a mystic. Kalu left his doors and windows wide open round the clock. He appeared very comfortable but with no visible means of livelihood. He appeared a happy man.

Neighbours said Kalu had no family; relation or friend. He was an easy-going loner who was found always cooking and cleaning his house. He hated dirt with passion-Kalu loved alcohol. He was seen as a good fellow.

In the evenings he was seen in drinking joints drinking and buying drinks for people. He drinks till well after mid night. Kalu met Obi. Their acquaintance took firm root in a few months before Adim left the city.

Many were surprised that Kalu who smiles all the time and a man that appeared not bothered by any challenge took Obi into his house.

CHAPTER TWELVE

Adaeke's death after a brief illness marked a turning point in the life of the Maduka's family. For Ajulu, it was a season of pain and sorrow.

Adaeke's daughters were united in demanding from Ajulu why they were not in the know about their mother's bad health condition. They suspect foul play in the death of their eighty-four year old mother. Ajulu's explanation to the effect that Adaeke only complained of headache and took two tablets of panadol shortly before going to bed only to be found dead the following morning fell on deaf ears.

The family and natives were thrown into confusion when all concerted efforts made to reach Obi with a view of getting him to come home and organize his mother's funeral failed. As a consequence, a delegation of three led by Adim was sent to Lagos to go break the sad news of Adaeke's death to Obi and bring him back home.

Making series of enquiries the delegates were led to Kalu's house. The Adim-led delegation was surprised to discover that at past nine at night no one was at Kalu's house even when the windows and doors were wide open.

A neighbour encouraged the men from Ani-Ugo to wait for Kalu noting that there was nothing unusual about what they saw.

"The man you've come to see is the strangest fellow we know. We hold him in awe. It may interest you to know that he is over seventy. He has no wife or children. No one knew where he came from or any of his relations or friends except for one funny fellow, Obi who moved in with him recently. Kalu has no visible means of livelihood yet he spent money as he wished. He is jovial, friendly and very kind but we all think that there is something about him that defiles human understanding Exercise patience. He surely would come back today."

Anxiety reached its highest pitch when at midnight Kalu did not come back. As Adim was sounding his men out as to what to do, they heard someone laugh aloud from a shouting distance. Moments later, the white beared Kalu walked casually into his house.

For a brief moment, Kalu stood gazing at the visitors who were seated in his living room. Beaming with smile he greeted them with warm hand shake without uttering a word. Kalu disappeared into his room and brought out water and some bottles of beer for his visitors.

"Have this while I quickly prepare food for you. I know you've waited for long and must be hungry now," Kalu said.

A thoroughly fidgety, Adim would not want to eat in the strange man's house. He wanted to finish the business that brought them to Kalu's house and leave immediately.

"Thanks my....my....brother. We're not....not hungry," Adim stammered. He appeared to have read the mind of his men. They nodded in unison.

"All well and good," Kalu replied.

Adim unveiled their mission to Kalu who responded with loud laughter. Adim and his men were confused. They never knew what caused Kalu's strange behaviour. They cast surprised glance at each other.

"Don't wear mournful looks for a woman that transited to higher glory a few days ago. You should be joyous that she is free at last from the grief, pain and sorrow of this world. She is now in a plane where there is no pain, sorrow, sickness or death... where there is night...and where love reign supreme. Weep not for her because she is happy and radiates love in her present state. Pray that you join her soonest to enjoy this bliss," Kalu beaming with joy told a thoroughly frightened Obi's Kinsmen.

"But ..... But.....where is Obi... I... I... We mean the dead woman's son. We understand he lives with you. We want to take him with us to go perform his mother's funeral in line with our custom. He's the woman's only son. And… And our people are anxiously waiting for him," Adim stammered.

Kalu laughed loudly for a brief moment and suddenly became calm before speaking coldly to visibly frightened visitors.

"Obi, a young man with chaotic lifestyle left this house at first cock crow one morning and never returned. That was three weeks ago," Kalu announced raising the temperature of tension in the air.

"Left for where?" Okonkwo, a member of the delegation asked worriedly. He was clearly disheartened.

"Well! I'm afraid he had gone to the way of all flesh. Obi has departed this world. He's dead. He is in harmony with his mother now. This is the plain truth. It is of no use beating about the bush or concealing the truth," Kalu dropped the bomb shell. His remark appeared to have heralded the first cock crow. Adim and his Kinsmen were speechless and numb. Shock and disbelief were written on their faces.

In Ani-Ugo Community, Adim-led delegation reported to their people that Obi was no where to be found in the city. Confusion and anxiety reigned supreme. Was Obi alive or dead became a question that agitated people's mind.

The oracle was consulted severally. The Oracle

said that Obi was dead. He was a victim of ritual killing. Adaeke was buried unsung.

Six months later, Obi's funeral commenced in line with tradition. Ajulu mourned her husband for a period of one year. Thereafter, the family burden weighed heavily on her with four step-daughters to cater for. Though abandoned to fate by her sisters-in-law she resolved to press forward. Ajulu made every sacrifice and worked to bare bones to keep her husband's family up and running.

CHAPTER THIRTEEN

Ajulu worked hard to cater for her step-daughter-chika, Nneka, Ego and Amaka. The challenge arising from raising the girls was seen as another cross fate placed on her shoulders. Though an uphill task, she was determined to do her best. Ajulu made native soap, weaved and dye cloths, and made vegetable farm in efforts to make ends meet.

While Chika and Nueka had passion for education; Ego who saw studies as unnecessary burden took to weaving; Amaka preferred to do nothing. She hated work and embraced indolence. Amaka would watch her sisters do household chores. At fourteen, she would spend hours in the bathroom. Thereafter, she would make up, strayed into the neighbourhood and hangout with some idler youths. Amaka created many headaches for Ajulu.

On one occasion, having received series of complaints from some well wishers about Amaka's misconducts, Ajulu was very cross with her stepdaughter. For once she flogged Amaka. A few elderly women in the neighbourhood joined Ajulu to discipline the recalcitrant girl.Theytied her hands and used an egg to carry out traditional virginity test on Amaka which she failed. Angered the more, they gave Amaka what the villagers call pepper treatment. For Amaka, hell crashed on his head. She wept uncontrollably. Amaka called on her dead mother, Comfort to come to her rescue. As Amaka writh in pain, Ajulu was moved to tears. She was worried whether the beating they gave Ajulu was excessive. She decided to pacify her.

"Amaka my daughter, it's my sacred duty to inculcate right values in you. I've often told you that life of indolence is no life at all. To choose to be a loafer amounts to attracting bad name to yourself and our family. Besides, you're a girl. If care is not taken, men would take advantage of you. A girl child ought to be homely and virtuous. I advise you to change for the better. I advise you as a mother who loves you dearly….."

"You….You're not….not my mother. My mother is…is…dead. You don't love me. You… you hate me".

Ajulu was shocked to her marrow at Amaka's outburst. She was determined to work hard in order to earn her trust.

Two years later, Amaka was put in the family

way. She did not know who was responsible for her pregnancy. Amaka gave birth to twin all boys. Meanwhile, Obi's Kinsmen were happy for it. To them, in line with Ani-Ugo tradition, Amaka's children belonged to Obi. They were glad Maduka's lineage would be up and running.

Five years on, Ego, nineteen was married to Okeke, a local Chief in the village of Ukah. Chief Okeke, sixty five, and pot bellied were a rich man and the biggest farmer in Ukah. He loved palmwine and women. Ego was his tenth wife; the youngest and the apple of his eyes.

Amaka who refused to breast feed his five months babies practically abandoned them. She went to live with her elder sister, Ego, in her new home. It did not take long before Amaka seduced the barely literate Okeke. Amaka and Okeke started having secret amorous affairs that resulted in Amaka being put in family way.

Ego was devastated when someone blew the lid open. She felt her younger sister betrayed her, and in fact had inflicted on her the deepest cut ever. Feeling very hurt she regretted ever knowing Amaka. Hell was let loose between the sisters. Ego hurriedly went to report the matter to her people. Many were shocked and condemned in the strongest terms Amaka's conduct. Others considered Amaka's misdeed as taboo and sacrilegious.

A few natives were at sea when a few months later Chief Okeke paid his way through and get Ani-Ugo people's consent to marry Amaka. Many knew

Okeke and his men had gone round to see the elders with money and bottles of gin.

"Our in-law-to-be, we all know that you are a great in-law. Make no mistake; we all understood why you got hooked to yet another daughter of ours. Is it not said that when a particular road is good, you ply it again and again? Go, rest assured of my full support," an elderly man who was very excited with the gift that Chief Okeke gave him. The man's teenage son, Uzo, was very disappointed at his father. He could not understand why his father who condemned Amaka's conduct and an elder who ought to be repository of integrity was quick to be corrupted. The elders were quick to abandon the letters and spirit of tradition they claim to uphold at the sight of gift. Uzo was at a loss why the elders pretend not to know that their evil ways were visible and known to all inspite their conspiracy of silence.

At the traditional wedding ceremony, Amaka clad in expensive white lace looked very happy. She appeared to be the happiest woman in the world. Amaka lighted the occasion with smiles. She could not understand why Ajulu and her company of hypocrites' wore heavy faces as if a funeral procession was going on. Amaka refused to care about how they felt. To her, it wastheir own cup of tea. As far as she was concerned, Okeke and herself were happy. Amaka was glad that Okeke, father of thirty six children had assured all and sundry that he could take good care of twenty wives and more.

Amaka wondered why some people were crying more than the bereaved.

A few weeks later Amaka took her twin babies to Okeke's house. Chief Okeke had agreed to be their foster father.

While Chika was admitted to a nursing school, Nneka was on the verge of completing her N.C.E course. As the challenges arising from their education continued to mount by the day, Ajulu was in dire stress. With help coming from nowhere, Ajulu in company of Chika went to the market one day to sell some of her wrappers to enable her buy some recommended books for Chika.

As Ajulu enquired from a friend whether she was interested in buying the clothes, the woman was mad at her. She chastised Ajulu in low tone for slaving for her step-daughters' education.

"Ajulu, are you out of your mind? What do you think you're doing? Why are you slaving for your late husband's children? Is it not said in Ani-Ugo that it's an effort in futility training other people's children. Why not learn from other people's experience that in fullness of time were paid with ingratitude. I tell you my friend yours wouldn't be any different."

"Thank you for your advice. I'm guided by my conscience. Providence made my step-daughters my own children. God entrusted them to my care. I'll do all I can to cater for them. I do all I do for the sake of God and humanity. I'll thread on this path for as long as I've the strength to carry on. It doesn't really matter whether any of my children takes care of me in my old age or not. God will always make a way," Ajulu replied.

Unknown to the women, Chika heard them clearly. She was happy with Ajulu. She vowed within her to support her step-mother as soon as she was gainfully employed. She saw in Ajulu a real mother who sacrificially loves her children.

Chika resolved to work hard inspite all odds so as to be somebody in future. Chika in her quiet moments had always prayed for a good relationship with her creator; a happy married life and a successful career that would provide her all the comfort of life.

CHAPTER FOURTEEN

Chika was in her final year in nursing school when she fell in love with Joseph. The young man was of the men who came in drove from the USA at Christmas period in desperate search for nurses to marry.

Chika's traditional married was fast tracked that in six weeks it was done. Joseph had insisted that he had no time on his hand. The ceremony was done in absentia as she was in the middle of her final examination.

Like most young women, Chika, twenty four was happy that she had gotten married. However, she was disturbed that she did not know Joseph well enough to have contracted the union. She saw her decision as risky. Meanwhile, Joseph, a man in his mid thirty appeared to be the happiest man in the world. Joseph had little formal education, and without a vocation/trade survived in the USA by doing odd jobs. He saw a gold mine in Chika. He used all means, fair and foul to convince Chika to accept his marriage proposal. Joseph had to give Chika good life that no man could match. He lied to Chika that he lived in a high brow area of Los Angeles; and a stone throw from Hollywood. Joseph said he lived in a mansion only a few could afford and had six state-of-the-art sport utility vehicles in his fleet of cars.

Initially, Chika was inwardly excited about the marital bliss she would have with Joseph that she did not think twice before accepting Joseph's hands in marriage. Not even the cautioning advice by Ajulu changed anything.

"My daughter, I'm happy for you. Marriage is every woman's dream. Nonetheless, there is something about your suitor that I don't seem to understand. Joseph appears to be hiding something. I'll strongly advice you don't accept his hands in marriage with the speed of light. You should rather take your time to investigate him the more. Yes, do a proper check on him. A man that puts on ear rings and plaits his hair like a woman, aside chewing gum must have curious character."

"I understand what you're drawing at but Mama Joseph is my dream husband. I've come to love him with all my heart and being. Besides, he lives in the USA, I mean God's own country! What could be better than that? He means the world to me; Chika replied with a thin smile.

"So going to America is the motivating factor in all this? You've turned blind eyes to his strange characters. Anyway, I still insist you do a thorough check on Joseph."

"Mama, my mind is made up about him,"

Months after Chika left for America, Nneka got married to Chief Kika, a crafty but notable politician in the locality. An N.C.E holder, Nneka was employed by the State Civil Service Commission as a teacher under the Ministry of Education. Nneka was posted to Igodo Grammar School located in her husband's home town.

Ani-Ugo was pissed off one fateful day when Amaka was paraded stack naked round the major streets in the community under scorching sum by a group of women called the Umuada. Amaka was painted in white chalk. They were on a cleansing exercise trip for Amaka who committed adultery, a serious taboo in the land.

The Umuada trailed Amaka singing abusive and mocking songs., armed with long canes, the women barked orders at Amaka which more often than not were obeyed reluctantly. She was driven by fear that her tormentors might flog her mercilessly. Children and adults soon joined the Umuada in their task of spiritual cleanings.

"Walk fast you good-for-nothing woman. You're a disgrace to womanhood. How dare you be in your husband's house and yet sleeping around with boys young enough to be your children?" A woman asked in an angry tone.

"Don't mind the wayward woman. She wants her husband and children to die prematurely. Nemesis has caught up with you." Another woman added.

"Amaka, may the gods punish you for subjecting us to this pain of walking this long distance under this biting sun all because you could not control your craving," Yet another woman remarked.

Ukachi, a woman passer-by stood for moments watching the women folks as they humiliate one of their own. She could not but wonder why there was so much hypocrisy in the world. She knew a few among the Umuada who were guilty of the offense Amaka committed except that they had not been caught red-handed. As far as Ukachi was concerned, Amaka was only unlucky to have been caught. For this singular reason she sympathized with Amaka. Also, Ukachi was sad that the women folks were at the forefront in destroying one of their own unlike men who would strenuously protect their own gender. Ukachi wondered why the boy that commited the said adultery with Amaka was shielded or perhaps given a tap on the wrist by the men. Being a voicelessmember of the society by reason of gender. A helpless Ukachi shrugged and moved on.

It was curious to many to note that Chief Okeke bluntly refused to heed the advice of some Kinsmen to send Amaka packing for sleeping with his nineteen year old house boy. However, Chief Okeke fearing for his life agreed that Amaka should be subjected to rigorous spiritual cleaning process as prescribed by custom for an unfaithful wife. Until that was done Okeke refused to eat Amaka's food or sleep in the same room with her. Many who knew Amaka were in no way surprised at the turn of events.

CHAPTER FIFTEEN

It was joy unspeakable for Ajulu when she was issued with a USA Visa by the United States embassy in Lagos. This was on the invitation of Amaka who was on the verge of putting to bed. Ajulu was full of hope and expectation because of her impending journey to America.

Ajulu had heard a lot of stories about America. Many of them seemed unbelievable. She had always wondered why anyone would want her to believe that in this foreign land, USA, there were thousands of ten storeys' and above buildings doting the streets and adoring the sky; uninterruptable water and power supply; more than eight lane roads, and many more. Ajulu would not stop wondering about the 'wonder' machine called the aeroplane, a product natives believe was product of white man's witch craft. Ajulu could not wait fly in this bird-like object that flies in the cloud, and thousands of feet above the sea level.

Five days before Ajulu travelled to America,

she bought and packaged twenty five tubers of yam, twenty five kg of garri, ten kg of palm oil and large quantities of dry fish, egusi, ogbono, pap, pepper soup spices, and ordered palm wine among other items.

The day before Ajulu was slated to travel to America, she spent major part of the day plainting her hair and receiving friends, relations and well wishers who stopped by her house to wish her safe journey. The journey had long become an important news across the community. A few seized the opportunity their visit provided to tell Ajulu all they have heard about America. They asked her to kindly confirm them upon her return.

"I understand that some roads are built in the space. Also, I understand some houses touch the cloud," Chinyere Ajulu's bosom friend said in utter disbelief.

"Yes ooh, my sister! I was even told darkness does not fall in that white-man's country," Uju added.

"Some even said over there they don't have kinsmen Yes! I was told Americans don't have Umunna or Umuada. Aggrieved natives go to the police and the court to settle even domestic differences. To make matter worse, we're told parents can't discipline their children. Also, I was told no one goes to his neighbour to request for fire wood, vegetable or salt. It's a case of everyone for himself. What a nonsense life style!" Anna lamented.
Peter, a middle aged relation of the Madukas, was

detailed to take Ajulu to the international airport in Lagos. Peter was a driver in Community secondary school where Nneka works. He preferred to be called senior driver because of long work experience. Many trusts Peter would perform the task well. He was seen as a bold and courageous person. His ability to speak passable English Language he learnt by interaction gave him comfort.

On the day of departure neighbours were right on hand to help Ajulu load her luggage in the twenty one year 18-seater mini school bus. With a short prayer said, Peter headed for Lagos, a journey that took nine hours.

They arrived at the departure hall of Murtala Mohammed International Airport, Ikeja, Lagos at about 4pm. After enquiry, they headed for 'check in' counter where a uniformed ground staff of the airport company told them that the counter would be opened for the checking in of passengers at 6pm. The gentlemen threw a surprised glance at Peter and Ajulu wondering in loud silence why Ajulu wants to travel with a mountain of luggage when thirty two kilogramme luggage was officially approved for an intending passenger. His eyes wandered in confusion. He decided to hold his peace until the appropriate time.

Not knowing where to go to while away time till 6pm Ajulu and her guardian, Peter, decided to stay put in the departure hall of the airport. They were happy their mission was on course.

With power outage, the hall became extremely hot. A few improvised for fan as sweat wet their clothes. Pressed, and hungry and yawning, Ajulu threw a few question at Peter.

"I'm pressed. But it appears there is no bush around here where one could urinate?"

Aaah! Noooo! Nothing like that here. This is an airport where white people land."

"But I'm pressed. Yes. I want to urinate. Or am I expected to urinate in my clothes?"

"Aunty, you've to try and control it ooh! People here may take you for a bush woman."

Take me for a bush woman for wanting to urinate? So people who work at the airport don't urinate? Well! God is on the throne."

"I'm hungry too. Where can we get plates, spoons and water to take some garri? At least we have garri with us," Ajulu asked yawning.

"Aaah! This is an airport. Such a thing is not allowed here. Police could even arrest us and throw us into cell."

Awooh! God forbid bad thing. I'd rather remain hungry. I don't want to miss this opportunity to go to America," Ajulu replied in clear pannick.

As soon as the counter was opened for intending passengers to start checking in, Ajulu fell in line. She was the second person in the queue. Many watched in silent surprise as Peter battled to gather Ajulu's mountainous luggage together. She became the Cynosure of all eyes.

Upon weighing Ajulu's luggage the airline ground staff told her they weighed seven hundred and fifty Kilogrammes. He told Ajulu that she was entitled to thirty two Kilogramme.

Moving on to the Custom's section, the four officers on duty cast a surprised glance at one another. Untieing the sacks in quick succession to Ajulu's discomfort, a Custom Officer ventured to ask:

Mama, what do you do with palmwine?"

Ajulu explained that her mission to America was to take care of her daughter and her grandchild that was expected to be born in a few days. What the natives call 'Inne Umugwo'. She stated that palmwine would assist her daughter's breast milk to flow well.

"Mama, you've palm oil, garri, fufu, pap, ogbono yam and…and….oh Gosh; I'm afraid you can't travel with any with these items.

Ajulu jumped in low alarm. Devouring the Custom Officer with her eyes. She made to tongue lashed the officer but realized she had not the words strong enough protest the officers position. Ajulu quickly turned to Peter for assistance.

"Peter, ask them in the language they would understand whether these food items are poison? Ask them whether their parents did not raise them with the same food stuff. Ask them whether it's a crime in the whiteman's land to eat our local food. If it's, tell them to remind the whiteman that big men in our land eat their food here and in fact are addicted to them, and use it as status symbol and no one had sent them to jail. What nonsense!" Ajulu lost her cool prancing the floor. It did not matter to her what tens of intending passenger behind her thought. She felt ill-treated.

As a few minutes after midnight Ajulu was airborne.

Her seat mate, Nkem, a middle aged woman assisted Ajulu a great deal. Aside helping to fasten her belt, Nkem got a hostess to take Ajulu to the convenience. It was Nkem who gave Ajulu the needed copany while the passengers that departed Lagos were awaiting a connecting flight to the USA in another country. Ajulu could not sleep for a moment. She wondered why fellow passengers could afford to catch a sleep when the Airbus 800 conveying hundreds of them appeared to be flying from one attitude to a higher one. Ajulu died many times when the Captain of the aircraft left the cockpit to exchange brief pleasantries with some passengers.

CHAPTER SIXTEEN

At the arrival hall of J. F. Kemedy's International Airport in New York, Ajulu tendered all her travel documents to the Immigration Officers, most of whom looked like giants.

She noticed an officer flip through her international passport and gaze at her at the same time. Ajulu's finger prints were taken. Ajulu was egged on to another table. A woman officer took her to a room where she was fisked. Some naira notes Ajulu carefully put inside her brazaie were brought out. Ajulu was sad and indeed could not understand why this cheerful uniformed woman young enough to be her daughter searched and almost stripped her. She wondered whether the young woman officer could do it to her mother. Ajulu was at a loss as to why visiting another man's land had caused her much pain, insult and humiliation.

Boiling on the inside, Ajulu wished she understood the white man's language.She would have tongue-lashed the woman officer for committing the abominable act on her.

Chika and Joseph were right on hand at the airport to receive Ajulu. Chika gave her a bear-hug. Joseph was happy that a mother who would gladly attend to Chika and baby's needs had come.

"Mama, I hope you enjoyed your flight?" Ajulu asked excitedly.

"My daughter, I don't think so! I had night-mare for the duration of the long journey. I tell you, I'm yet to recover from it. But the wizardry of the whiteman is a case study. For goodness sake how could a small bird-like object freight hundreds of people and the luggage with ease in the cloud? My heart was in my mouth all the while because had the machine developed fault where would they effected repairs? In the air? I tell you, God gave the white man unique gifts. In fact, he is God in his right. Other races merely accompanied him to the world.

"Aaaah Mamaaah! Well, I'm not going to en-gage you in any argument right away. Lets get home first for you to eat and rest. You look tired and hun-gry. Mama I hope you eat on board?"

"Noo! My daughter! They didn't serve us any food. I requested for pounded yam or fufu with egusi soup but they said they had none of them. What they gave us as food was only good for chil-dren. It would cause me stomach upset. Don't forget there is no latrine in the cloud. Even before we left Lagos, it took the camel to pass through the eye ofa needle before a woman showed me where to urinate. My daughter, I almost wet my clothes."

Chika and Joseph exchanged surprised glances. Chika knew her step mother must have passed through hell to reach America due to ignorance. She vowed to educate her about air travel.

With increased heart beat Ajulu gazed at sky scrapers on their way home. She was dumbfounded about the road network. She began to confirm fewthings people had said about America.

A few weeks in America, even though she was provided with all she needed but Ajulu appeared a sad person. She failed to understand the values of the white man. Chike who had been uncomfortable with her step-mother's countenance enquired from her one day what was amiss. Ajulu had hissed without meaning it.

Mama, anything the matter? Why are you hissing? I noticed you've not been happy since you came here three weeks ago. Yes, you've always been moody. Did my husband or I offend you in anyway?" Chika asked.

"Nothing is the matter my daughter. Nobody offended me. Perhaps, I've been angry with the way people live here.Every one appeared to mind his business. It bruised my psyche because this is not the way of our people. Night has been drowned by it." Ajulu replied.

"How do you mean, Mama?"

"Oooh, you don't know?" Ajulu asked with disgusting rage. "Allwell and good! Now tell me my dear daughter, why is it that on the day I arrived here children in the neighbourhood didn't rush in here to hog and welcome me not even the children of your next door neighbor. There was no child to give the coconut I brought from home.

Tell me why did your next door neighbor aside ignoring me walked leisurely into his car with his family and drove away? I want to know why the elderly women in this neighbourhood haven't been flowing into your house to rejoice with us on the arrival of our new baby boy and perhaps help out with the bathing of mother and child. Is the arrival of a baby no longer a bundle of joy in the community? Why are they not preparing pounded yam and pepper soup for you as a nursing mother? Why did they abandon you to fate? Why do you all abhor visiting each other but prefer talking by that box like object?

Why... why? Ajulu was choked because she had many questions.

"Mamaaah!Mamaa!" Chika interrupted her step mother

"Don't Mama me! Tell me if this community excommunicatedyou. Tell me what your offenses are that we may take Kolanut and palmwine and go beg elders and titled men in this land .You can't be an Island onto yourself or can you? Tell me..."

"Mamaaa! It's not what you think. It's not like that.

It ......"

"It's not like what? Then what is it like? Am I blind not to see? Look Chika! You've changed a great deal. In fact, I'm beginning to suspect you."

"Mama, the truth is that your observations were right but it's just the way people live here. Our cultural values are remarkably different. There is no communal life the kind we know back home. Here, everyone is for himself."

"Errrh! God save His people! My dear daughter, I've heard enough for the day. I don't want to worsen my heartache.Let's talk about this serious matter another day."

Day in day out, Ajulu continued to think about this land called America; where people spoke through their nose; land that houses millions of high rise building; a land that had many roads lanes; land of giants; a land that never saw darkness nor sleep; a land where self interest drives his action; a land where everyone is answerable to the laws of the land and a land where.....

Ajulu became very uncomfortable when she tried each morning but could not find farmers go to their farms with their cutlasses and hoes. All she saw was thousands of neatly dressed people dashing out to work every morning only to come back in the evening still looking neat. Ajulu wondered what manner of work they do not get their clothes dirty. She saw men women go to work round the clock.

With a rumbling stomach, Ajulu shrugged. "What a land!What a people! What a world!" she murmured.

Ajulu resolved to ignore the 'abominable' values of American Society and face the task that brought her to America- Inne Omugwo.

Ajulu was happy that the 'bad people' at the airport did not confiscate her soup spies. She was sad her palmoil, yam tubers, garri and palmwine were seized.

Ajulu was deeply sad that Chika could not produce adequate breast milk for her baby. She coursed the people who seized her palmwine and pap. Her anger heightened when Chika began to introduce baby friendly on the ground that she would resume work in a few days. Chika equally made it clear to her that she was not disposed to feeding her three-month baby with exclusive breasting for six months. This caused a heated argument between Chika and her step-mother.

"Mama, I'll be resuming works in a few days. My husband and I have decided to do our son's dedication the day after next at our church. So, I'll like us to go and shop for what we'd wear. Also, we'd buy things we'd use to entertain our guests," Chika told Ajulu one morning.

"My daughter, how could you resume work when your baby is only three months old. Who would be breast feeding him?"

"It's the condition of my work. Yes. My employer's rule"

"Your employers must be wicked. I hope you're not about to abandon your home in the name of going to work like your absentee husband who dashes in and out of the house always claiming to be on duty. But I was not born yesterday. I know what men do. Yes, I know their past time. Let me ask again, how will you breast feed my grandson?"

"Mama, I'll always press and store my breast milk for my baby. It'll be refridgeted and you could give him as and when necessary."

"Abomination! Press and store breast milk? For who?My grandchild? What is this world turning?"

"But Mama that is the practice here. We, the nursing mothers, can't afford to abandon our various careers to wean our babies on exclusive breast feeding. Thanks to baby food that came to our rescue.

"Now, I can confirm this is a crazy society. Here you do things as they please you. By the way, what do say you want to do the day next to tomorrow?".

"Mama, we're doing our baby's dedication in my church we'll be naming and dedicating our baby to God on that day."

"But it's the elders and men in the community that ought to name the baby. Why are you turning custom on its head?"

"Mama, the child's naming will be done in the church on Sunday. He'll be named Emmanuel – God is with us. It's a name I carefully chose for him. Isn't it a fine name?"

"Taboo! How could you, a woman, be choosing a name for your baby when in actual fact is the duty of your husband and elders of the community. And by the way, how would you get the elders of the community to agree to go to the church to perform the child's naming ceremony? How would they comfortably use kola-nut, white chalk, palmoil, salt, dry fish and other items to perform the rites in the church without the owners of the church complaining? Have you informed the women folk in this community? To come help with the cooking, and thereafter dance in their traditional attire? Besides, have you chosen, brought and distributed Ashuabi (uniform) to your friends for the occasion?"

"Mamaaa! We don't need elders and items you mentioned for my child's dedication and naming ceremony. The church will not allow anything fetish. Yes! The church will not torch with a long pole kolanut and all what not. It's primitive."

"What is primitive eeh? What nonsense are you talking about? Anyway! I don't have time to listen to you because you're merely celebrating your ignorance. Your values here are distorted. It's sad and I consider it very sad to think of the emptiness of life in America despite her beauty and splendour."

Two days later Chika did her child's dedication and naming ceremony it took place in the church-Saints Mission Church Inc. some friends of the Josephs including four women accompanied them to the church.

The guests, seven in number, eat lightly,

drank soda and water, and in ninety minutes were all gone. Ajulu on her own named her grandchild Chukwuebuka-Ebuka for short. However, she grieved over the colourless naming ceremony and considered it a sham.

Ajulu vowed that she would henceforth ignore and accommodate the America values despite its ugly nature. She recalled being taught as a child to accept those things she cannot change, and that when one is in Rome he should behave as Romans. Ajulu was determined to make herself happy since she was in no position to change American Culture nor take its good sides only.

CHAPTER SEVENTEEN

Ajulu stayed five months and indeed was beginning to enjoy her stay when she was jolted by Chika one early morning. Her stepdaughter told her that it was about time they started making preparation for her to return to Nigeria.

A shocked Ajulu recalled she heard Chika and Joseph swim in joy over the two years visa the USA Embassy in Lagos issued her. Chika had given her a bear hug considering her a lucky woman. Ajulu remembered asking Chika what the excitement was all about and she was told that American government had given her the rare privilege of visiting their country for two years. For Ajulu, the past five months was like a blink of the eye.

Ajulu wondered why Chika and Joseph want her out of America, a country she was beginning to fall in love with despite her 'distorted' values.

Ajulu wondered what she had done wrong to warrant her being 'forced' back home. She could now understand why Chika and her 'queer' husband were chatting over dinner the previous evening in low tone. Cloud of disappointment flushed across Ajulu's face. She felt betrayed by her step-daughter. Taking a deep breath she dared to clarity some issues she appeared not to understand.

"My daughter, I should be getting prepared to go where?"

"Home, Mama. I mean to our native country."

"Why? I've only been here for five months! I thought you said I could stay for two years?"

"No, no , no Mama, your visa permits you to stay for only six months at a time but you could come again within the two years the visa remains valid. The immigration law doesn't permit you to stay beyond six months per trip. If you over stay, you may not be allowed entry into this great country in future. Mama, I tell you in this great country, the law is respecter of no one. All is equal before the law".

"Aaaah! Nooo! Devil is a liar. I'd rather leave to be able to come back in future. Is it not said my daughter by the ancients that he who fights and runs away lives to fight another day?"

"Very true, Mama."

"But you must promise that I won't be away for long."

"I promise, Mama!"

One night precisely at 11pm, Ajulu and Chika went to a chainstore that stretched hundreds of metres with every product appeared stored in it. Hundreds of people, young and old, were busy picking things off the shelf and putting them in their trorey. Ajulu wondered why no one greeted her "why do the youths despise the aged in this society?" she murmured.

At the payment point, Ajulu watched with confusion how the sales boys and girls, all armed with machines, enter the prices of items in her storey before summing it up. Generating a slip from the machine, the sales girl handed it to Chika who nodded with a smile before giving her a plastic card which the girl inserted into the machine.

"Why were you allowed to carry all these items away without payment or are you allowed to buy on credit here. Are you their good customer?.

"No! Mama, I've paid for the goods with my credit card.

"You did? But I didn't see you give them any money I mean cash.

"Mama, here we seldom pay for goods with cash. Or go about with so much money in our purse. This plastic has money in it. I paid with it."

"You've money in this card? Hmmm! Another America wonders!" Ajulu exclaimed.

She could not understand how a mere plastic had turned to money.

"If in American wisdom, mere plastic card serves money how come you did not bargain the prices of goods you bought. Or does the law forbid you from bargaining price of goods too?"

"Mama, in chain stores we don't. Every item has a price tag on it."

"Then why are you being wasteful. Why can't you go buy your things in an open market on a market day where you can negotiate prices? Yes, go to where market woman display their wares-fish, pepper, tomatoes and so on, and buy your things. There you bargain and get better value for your money."

"There is no such market here, Mama."

"Whaaat! Unbelievable! Then something is terribly wrong with this society," Ajulu yelled disappointedly. She decided to change the line of discourse.

"My daughter, I want to know who will take care of my grandson, Chukwuebuka when I leave and when you're at work."

"Oooh! You mean Emmanuel? My husband and I plan to hire a nanny. In the event that I'm not at home and our nanny is off duty, Joseph would baby-sit him. It's just that the services of nannies here are very expensive but we don't have a choice."

So, what you're telling me is that you'd be paying a stranger to be taking care of your child? Suppose she disappears with the baby for whatever reason. I wish there is a relation or fiend to help out."

"God forbid! In any case if such happens, I'm confident police and FBI will track and arrest her.

They will bring the full weight of the law to bear on her. Mama, this God's own country, America, has highly effective law enforcement agents. Besides, no one is above the law and criminals rarely escape justice.

Few days before Ajulu's departure Chika and Joseph had bought items that filled four large suit cases for her. The items include assorted shoes, clothes, toiletries and japery. A shirt was packaged for Peter in appreciation for his assistance to Ajulu

Despite all these, Ajulu was only half happy. She could not find Hollandies or George wrappers to show off with back home as someone who went to do 'Omugwo' again, she could not buy a bag salt and a basket of onions she would distribute the village women folks as was the practice. She wondered why her own 'Inne Omugwo' will be different from others. Aluju became sad Chika noticed her but knew she never offended her. She chose not to think or talk about it. To her, she had climbed the mountain to show appreciation to her step mother.

On the day Ajulu departed USA, Joseph was at work, Chika tied Emmanuel with the car's seat belt. With the assistance of Ajulu, Chika put her step-mother luggage into her car.

Mr. Woods, a lanky clean shaved and Chika's next door neighbour was mowing his lawn. He stood transfixed like a stone status gazing at Ajulu and step-daughter without saying a word.

"What does that man want from us?" Ajulu asked"

"Mama, leave him alone. He must be battling with his family challenges. Seven months ago, he was released from prison for beating his wife and only last week he was arrested, detained and charged to court for flogging his ten years old son. Mama, you know what? This is his fourth marriage. He pays alimony to three ex-wives."

"Imprisoned for beating his wife? Didn't he pay her bride price? And did you say he was also detained and charged to court for flogging his own child. Abomination! Is it not said by the ancients that he who spared the rod would spoil the child. What an arrant nonsense!"

"Mama, that is the law. You don't beat a child or woman in this society. They're not animals. Even animals are protected against extreme violence. Besides, men don't pay dowry here."

"Law my foot! Who knows whether the man's wife is not submissive to him. No wonder why children and women behave as they wish. Can't you see thousands of boys put on ear ring and girls walk the law that makes women and children untouchable? Why will you blame a man for divorcing three wives in a short while or for disowning their unruly children? Please don't spoil my day. You had better stay in your America and let me go back to my native land to live with my people. My psche is bruised by American value.

Ajulu hissed, spate on the ground and entered the car for onward journey to the airport. Chika could not understand why her step-mother was particularly angry with American culture. Yet, she desired to stay put. To her, it was an irony and one of the highest order.

CHAPTER EIGHTEEN

Ajulu was received on arrival at the Murtala Mohammed International Airport, Lagos by Peter. She could not leave for the village almost immediately as planned as her luggage arrived two days later.

The unapologetic airline officials kept on asking her and her fellow passengers to come back and check the next day.

Ajulu was saddened by the frequent power outage and lack of portable water in Nigeria. She was depressed by pot holes infested roads she plied while going back to the village.

At Ani-Ugo, Ajulu was given a rousy welcome. Drums were practically rolled out by the young and the old. This gladdened Ajulu's heart. Unknown to her, Peter had leaked the information about her arrival from the USA. A few who waited anxiously were disappointed about her failure to come back on the appointed day.

Ajulu did her best to ensure that the goodies she brought from America, such as biscuits; sweets, peanuts and chocolate reached everyone. Many were happy they tasted the goodies. The feeling of self-importance overwhelmed Ajulu. In her carriage she made effort to ape the Whiteman.

The following evening, with Ajulu feeling terrific; in her sparsely furnished living room were tens of natives whose motive was to see the goodies they could still get from a woman who had seen the world.

Peter took it upon himself to pilot the affairs of the informal gathering. A few told Ajulu all what happened in the village while she was away. Thereafter, some threw questions at Ajulu about America. Others tried to confirm some things they have heard about America.

"Mama! Mama! Is it true that Ame..Ameri. America is as beautiful as the pictures we see in the television in Ike's house show.Mama, is it also true that…….." Oli asked and meant to continue but Peter cut her short angrily.

"Hey, hey, stop! How dare you address our own Mama America as ordinary Mama? I mean a lady that just came back from our modern day promised land. Is it a mean feat? No one can ignore or wish this fact away. Enough of this insult!"

"I'm sorry."

"You had better be."

"My sister, the beauty and splendour of America is indescribable. Yes, mouth can't describe it. Where would I start?Is it the hanging roads; buildings that touch the cloud; tap that flow or electricity that is supplied all day? I tell you, seeing in believing!"

"Ajulu replied feeling good.

"Do they know about us in that part of the world?"

"Yes they do. They call us Africans. Sadly, our image is prejudiced. Information manages don't informed Americans right about Africa. The news about us talks mainly about war, famine, poverty, natural disaster, disease, savagery, superstition, idolatry and so on and so forth."

Mama...Oh, sorry, I mean Mama America, please tell us as a fellow woman if it's true that in America woman marry women, and some men marry men. Is it not abomination? Don't they have taboo over there?"

"Hmmmm! It's true. In some states inAmerica men marry fellow men and women marry women legally. They have no shame. They parade themselves in public place. The court and churches wed them and in fact issue them with marriage certificates. Even my daughter's male neighbour married his male friend......." Ajulu said but was interrupted by a hot tempered Eze.

"Taaah! Abomination, taboo, sacrilege,..." Eze yelled.

"What a minute. I've not finished," Ajulu

said "Even where the marriage is between a man and a woman, the woman always claims equal right with her husband. They share household chores. If the woman cooks today, the man would cook the next day. In most cases, the man is always left to wash the dishes, sweep, scrub the floor and wash his wife's clothes. Yes, men do domestic chores. Law enforcement agents are quick to throw them into cell for disciplining their wife or children. Women place their career above marriage. Look, it."

"Errrrh!But Mama… Mama America, why did the elders in their community allow such sacrilege, such sham, such abomination and such taboo. Don't they have culture and tradition?" Ada enquired.

"To be honest with you, that appears to be the most curious thing about America. I tell you, in America there is no Kingdom or Kings; Obi-in-council, Elders-in-council; Chief and Elders. Over there they don't have Kinsmen, agegradesor Umuada. Communal life is near zero. Everyone appears to be driven by self interest. It's all about I, me and mine. Their ways are as chilling as the cold over there."

"If they don't have Umunna, then, now do they settle quarrels among themselves? Who drinks the palmwine suitors bring to would-be-in-laws. Above all, how do they undatake the rite-of-passage of a dead relation?" Orji, a known traditionalist asked visibly worried by the ear blocking things he heard from Ajulu about America.

Smiling broadly with air of importance Ajulu responded.

"Well Elder Orji, in America people settle their differences in police stations and courts. Also, marriages are contracted in marriage registry and/or in the churches. It does not matter whether parents consent to their children's marriage or not. Besides, no palm wine is broughtto the bride's family. Also, no bride price is paid to the bride's family. In any case, there is no palm wine in America! Again, burials are done in public cemetery. The relations of the dead person may not even be involved"

"Errrh! There is no palm wine in America. May the gods of our father not take me there for even one day," Akama, a palm wine addict said.

"Ewoooo! Nnadi screeched his hands on the head." The ancients said that the eye do not see the ear. Surely their dead would not be resting in peace because proper rites-of-passage are not performed by family members. Why can't somebody teach them our time-honoured culture?"

"So, Mama…. Mama America, you mean the white man would also rely on government to clear foot paths to their farms and even sweep their markets?" An agitated Orji asked.

"In America, there are no foot paths to the farms. There, only a handful of people farm in large scale. I tell you farms owed by all farmers put together in Ani-Ugo are less than what one white farmer would cultivate with his machines. Besides, there are no open markets in America where sellers sent their wares and buyers go to buy, and even bargain prices. All they do is to go to chain stores and pick goods off the shelf with price tag on them. Buyers do not carry cash about.The pay with plastic money. I tell you America is a crazy society despite its beauty and splendour. The people there practically stood against our sacred tradition and custom".

"Yes, America is a crazy society. I think you're absolutely right. I think it more than crazy. My psych has been badly bruised tonight by American abominable values. I must leave immediately." Eze announced visibly angry.

As quickly as Eze stormed out of Ajulu's house, Orji followed suit. In no time everyone was gone. Many left with bleeding hearts following the 'abominable' stories they heard from a woman who saw it all about a land many people described to be, America.

CHAPTER NINETEEN

Four day after Ajulu came back to Ani-Ugo, thieves broke into her house. They carted away all she brought from America. Curiously, Ajulu who slept like someone sedated did not hear any noise. A rudely shocked Ajulu wondered in wild confusion how the thieves entered her house that was under lock and key without evidence of forcible entry. For her, a night of long suffering had begun.

Raising the alarm, neighbours gathered in Ajulu's house in split moment. Many were dumbfound by the havoc the thieves wreaked on Ajulu, the woman of the moment in the community.

"This is the handiwork of dare-devil criminals," sometochukwu noted.

"Yes! They are heartless bitches; another person added.

"If the doors were under lock and key, how come there was no evidence of forcible entry?" Okem asked.

"These crooks have Master keys that could open any door!" Nduka replied.

The startled natives were of the opinion that the thieves might not have come from Ani-Ugo.

"I want to believe that petty thieves in this community such as Adu and the rest of them who specialize in stealing of goats and chickens; yam and animals caught by people's trap, couldn't have committed this robbery. They have not grown in sophiscation as to rob this way," Okobi said.

Some empathetic callers understood Ajulu's pain. They consoled her. A few advised her that being a VIP in society by virtue of having visited America she deserved better personal security. They asked her to go to the neighbouring village of Ani-Ukwu and report the incident to the police. These people want the criminals to be quickly fished out, arrested, subjected to due process and sent to jail.

The news of Ajulu's robbery spread in the community like wild fire. From person to person and from place to place, the incident was painted in colours that suited the reports. Someone said that Ajulu was given the beating of her life by the robbers. Another person said that Ajulu was raped by the ten-man gang till she fainted. And yet, another person fuelled the rumour mill on the robbery incident by saying that the robbers forced. Ajulu to provide drinks and food for them before tying her to the bed, and robbed her.

The elders of Ani-Ugo reacted promptly to the robbery incident the type of which they had not witnessed in the community. The elders were angry that their dear daughter, Ajulu a woman of the world who had been to the white man's country and learnt the culture could be robbed by hoodlums.

In the emergency meeting summoned to discuss the matter the same ay tempers went wild as speaker after speaker spoke in condemnation of the robbery. It was resolved that everyone-man, woman, boy and girl should assemble at the village's Ndichie (an ancestral shrine) at 7am the next day to levy curses on the perpetrators of the heinous crime against Ajulu a woman that brought honour to the community. Traditional worshippers were expected use the instruments of worship to rain curses on the robbers, other faith based bodies were asked to use their holy books to pray dangerous prayers against the criminal.

The turnout of people was impressive. Ajulu felt profoundly honoured and humbled. She shed tears of joy because of people out pouring of love. She did not know that she was so loved by her people.

From the Ndichie shrine the people marched round the major streets in Ani-Ugo heaping curses on the criminals who robbed Ajulu. A few refused to participate in the exercise. Some claim it was ungodly for people to curse fellow men for whatever reason. These people would rather prefer God to judge the criminals at His own time.

Five days later, the community was agog with the news that some of the thieves had been caught. One of the robbers who felt cheated while the spoils of their robbery were shared squealed. The youths quickly mobilized and arrested four of the thieves. The angry youths beat them blue black before handing them over to the police on the insistence of Ajulu. She told them that was civilized culture.

Upon police investigation two more thieves were arrested. Though it was shocking to all and sundry that five out of six robbers arrested were from neighbouring village, the bit of information that bent the minds of many locals was the one that confirmed that it was. Peter who gave information and duplicate keys to Ajulu's house to the robbers.

Peter had confessed to the police attributing his action to the handiwork of the devil. He begged for forgiveness from Ajulu, a woman she said was like a mother to him. The matter was promptly charged to court. The trial lasted six months. At the end, Peter and his co-travellers were found guilty of the offense as charged. They were sentenced to five years in prisonment with hard labour.

CHAPTER TWENTY

With Ajulu's stolen property held in the court as exhibit while the matter lasted, life was tough for her. Ajulu had sleepless nights thinking on what to do in order to eke out a living

She resolved to go back to farming and cloth weaving, her familiar tuff. Also, Ajulu, 65, alias Mama America was determined to get some basic education especially in the use of English Language. She wanted to speak for herself in any forum. Ajulu hated relying on a third party to speak her mind. She knew no one could talk for her exactly the way she would to express herself. The need to learn English Language had become more compelling now that Peter was cooling his left in prison. Ajulu registered in the Adult Education programme that was introduced in Ani-Ugo by the government. The local folks called the programme Evening School.

A few weeks later, Ajulu, with the little money in her possession engaged two labourers who brushed part of her late father-in-laws farm land. On her way to the farm one early morning, some natives were shocked to see her on the foot path to the farm.

Two women carrying heavy load of baskets of cassava greeted Aluju. They exchanged surprised glances at each other. The women wondered what someone who had been to America was going to do in the farm.

"Is that not Ajulu. I mean Mama America! Or are my eyes deceiving me?" Lucy asked Ndidi

"She sure is. I almost jumped out of my skin when I saw her!"

"Yes, even me! My heart almost sank into my belly.

"Where is she off to?" Lucy asked.

"She is going to the moon! For goodness sake, you saw someone on the foot path to the farm and you're asking me where she is going," Ndidi replied.

"What business does Mama America have on the farm? This is a woman who had gone to the white man's country what a share?".

"This is strange my sister. I tell you Mama America's action is both degrading as it's shameful. It's clear that Mama America has no sense of self-worth at all.My heart bleeds."

"Very well! Let her continue to compete with

us for the right of way in the bush. Shameless woman!"

"Well, that is her funeral!"

The women expressed anti Ajulu biases and continued their homeward bound journey.

Ajulu took the negative criticisms trailing her going back to the farm in giant, stride. She believed that there was dignity in labour. She believed that only illegimate veatures were un-dignifying. Not wanting to listen to voices of ignorant people, Ajulu tilled the land to earn a living. She cultivated vegetable, cocoyam, maize and cassava among other crops in her farm.

Six months on the farm, fate worsened Aluju's condition. She stepped on stunt that gave her deep cut on her left toe. Swollen and reeling in deep pain, Aluju was taken to the hospital in the neighbouring town of Ukah. Aluju's cut was stitched. She was hospitalized for ten days. Doses of anti-tetamus injection were administered to her among other anti biotics drugs.

Upon her return, apart from Chika other step-children spoke in one voice. They asked their step-mother to stop farm work but she refused. Not until she was bitten by a snake, a crawling animal that Ajulu dreaded so much that she left the farm for good. Chika's strong worded letter from America requesting her once again to stop farming quickened Ajulu's decision. Ajulu did not want to hurt Chika's feeling otherwise her desire to visit America again might be jeopardized.

With Ajulu out of the farm, she threw her full weight into weaving of clothes. With six trainee-assistants teenage girls, Ajulu made a living from weaving and a comfortable one at that.

Ajulu surprised many when she registered in adult education class. Given the fact that she had travelled to the USA, she was placed a class above her peers. Ajulu was happy for it. She knew that even if no one had acknowledged the fact that she was ahead of her peers by virtue of her international exposure, stones would have risen to do so.

Ajulu, 68, was registered and placed in primary 2A. The school ran from 4.pm to 7.pm from Monday to Friday. Ajulu's class teacher, Mr. Obiora was a non-native who lived three houses away from Ajulu's. He addressed her as Mama America to Ajulu's delight. Ajulu's class mates soon followed suit.

Ajulu's passion to learn the white man's language, English Language made her spend almost all her study time on the subject. She participated actively in the class and was heard loudest during English Language lessons. Aside from asking countless questions she attempted answering all question posed by the teacher. Inspite this, Ajulu appeared not to be making good progress in the subject. Though her cow scores in home works, tests and examinations discouraged and demoralized her, she was determined never to give up in the understanding and usage of English language.

One fateful day, Mr. Obiora, during an English Language lesson had asked every pupil to make sentence with the following two, three and four letter words pronoun-He, she and they.

"To conclude the lesson of today, let me remind you and in fact engrave it in your memory that a noun is the name of any person, place or thing. Also, commit it to memory that a pronoun is a word used instead of a noun. Is it well understood?" Obiora asked

"Yes sir!" The class chorused.

"All well and good! Now, I want each and every one of you to make sentences with the follow pronounsHe, she and they.

As quickly as Obiora landed, Ajulu was on her feet; Giving Obiora a confident smile she set the floor rolling.

"Yes, Madam America, let's go!"

"My father is a he; my mother is a she, and all of us in this class are they."

"God have mercy! This is incredible! This is unbelievable," Obiora yelled. Disappointed and hands akimbo, he looked on helplessly even as the class rolled in uncontrollable laughter. In deep anger, Obiora brought the English Language lesson to a close.

Ajulu did not know what she said wrong that warranted the reaction. She felt unperturbed about it. Ajulu sat down girlishly in a manner that made Obiora go red. He thanked God that he was not permitted to discipline adult-pupils otherwise he would have given Ajulu the trashing of her life for that unpardonable blunder.

CHAPTER TWENTY ONE

Ajulu, 69 was happy she was promoted to primary four; though English language still gave her serious challenge Arithmetic was a nightmare to her. She begged to disagree with Obiora anything he told the class to develop more interest in arithmetic because it was both interesting and a living subject.

"I've always wondered why many of you have morbid hatred for an interesting and living subject as arithmetic. No living being can do without it. Whenever we're planting; building, buying selling, cooking, travelling and so on and so forth. We're consciously and unconsciously applying some arithmetic functions. I tell you, no one can operate effectively in today's world without having good knowledge of arithmetic, "Obiora had posited.

"I hear you!" Ajulu murmured.

The mere mention of arithmetic hurts Ajulu like hell. The lesson on fraction almost, pushed her to breaking point. The manipulation of figures in solving posers involving fraction almost made her run amork. The introduction of BODMAS as basic formula for solving fraction problems worsened her plight.

Unknown to Obiora, whenever he stood before the class to teach arithmetic Ajulu's heart sinks into her belly. Ajulu hated arithmetic with passion. She believed arithmetic was a demon that should be exorcised.

Ajulu over flowed with joy when Nneka came one fateful Sunday to inform her that her step-daughters had agreed to celebrate her seventieth birthday on a day she could choose and adopt as her birthday.

Smiling from check to check, Ajulu without voicing a word stood up and graciously walked into her bedroom. Appearing moments later with her international passport she handed the passport to Nneka who wondered what her passport had got to do with the issue she tabled.

"My dear Nneke, please flip through the passport and tell me the date I arrived America three years ago. I understand it's written in the document"

"Mama, but what has it got to do with the issue being discussed?"

"Do as I said, my daughter."

Nneka reluctantly took the passport from

her step-mother. Flipping through the passport, Nneka found Ajulu's arrival date, the USA' immigration authority stamped on the travelling document.

"Mama, you arrived in the USA on October 12," Nneka said.

"Are you sure?"

"Yes Mama. You can even confirm it yourself. At least you now go to evening school.

"Yes, you're right but it appears I've phobia for figures. They turn my eyes" Ajulu said paused a while. Smiling broadly she continued. "Nneka go tell my children that I've adopted October 12 as my birthday. It was the day that I came in contact with the world; found happiness liberty and human dignity and civilized values. It was on that day that I em....em...em," Ajulu said and meant to continue but she was axed by Nneka.

"Mamaaa! I did know you've fallen head over heels in love with America despite your strong condemnation of her cultural ethos upon return.

"Yes, I had my reservation about their values but reflecting on everything, I tell you that America is the final Bus-stop. In fact, if it's not America it can be like America. I tell you going to America marked a significant turning point in my life. My daughter go and tell my children and indeed the whole world that October 12 is my birthday. Though there was no birth registry at the time I was born I'm absolutely, certain that I was born on that date. God willed it and it's permanent."

When Nneka wrote in a letter to Chika her encounter with Ajulu, she rolled into bout of laughter. She decided to facilitate another trip for Ajulu to the USA if that would make her happy. She recalled that way back in time she vowed to take care of her step-mother.

Six months before October 12, plans were set in motion to give Ajulu a memorable seventieth birthday celebration. Nneka and her husband were the arrow heads. A notable caterer cum event manager was contracted. Also, two popular local musicians were contracted to perform during the party. Colourful invitation cards were made and who-is who in Ani-Ugo was invited. The invitation was extended to the Igwe who was the political traditional and spiritual head of Ani-Ugo community. His HRH's council members were equally invited. The local folks though not formally invited were full of expectation. In their informal gatherings the impending birthday party was thoroughly discussed.

When the long awaited day came, Aluju and natives were pleasantly surprised at the elaborate birthday ceremony Aluju's step-daughters organized for her. Immediately after the Thanks Giving Service in a church that ended at noon, the sun stood still for Aluju for the rest of the day.

The event took place in the only primary school premises in the community. The arrival of Igwe Azike and his chiefs electrified the venue of the party.

Musicians took their turn to perform in line with the deft MC's instruction. With two cows slaughtered for the occasion, food was in abundant supply. Assorted drinks flowed freely in all direction. The quests were feted.

Ajulu in custom made attire from the USA sat on a chair specially reserved for her. She looked queenly and was sandwiched between the Igwe and his chiefs and her step-daughters who wore the same colourfully made attire. Hundreds of photographs were taken. The quests exploded when a special number was played for the celebrant who displayed beautiful dance steps to the admiration of quests. As they danced their hearts out, there was money rain on Ajulu, the celebrant. Ajulu was touched by the over flowing emotion from her children. She shed tears of joy as certain thoughts about the past flashed her mind.

The ceremony reached its highest emotional pitch when a high ranking chief, speaking on behalf of Igwe Azike announced that the Igwe had decided to confer the chieftaincy title of Ezinne I of Ani-Ugo kingdom on Ajulu in recognition of her sacrificial and exemplary love, care and support of her step-daughters, symbol of mother hood and a woman of integrity.

Ajulu was asked to step forwards and the Igwe directed the same chief to anoint her feet with X local while chalk. Ajulu was asked to prepare for the investiture proper and as quickly as possible. Ajulu felt profoundly honoured by the Igwe and his council of Chiefs. She saw her matter as a case of moving from zero to heroin. To her, who would have imagined years back that a day like this would come.

Every guest got a beautiful mug, fez cap and a 'T' shirt with inscription "Happy birthday, dear sweet mother" as souvenir. Though it was a memorable occasion for all who were there, it was better still a significant lesson for all those women who were not lucky to have their own biological child.

Four days later Ajulu jetted out to America, a land she had fallen head over heel in love with.

ABOUT THE AUTHOR

Azuka Monyei

Azuka Monyei hails from Issele - Uku in Delta State of Nigeria. He had his first and secondary degrees in Economics and Business Administration respectively at the University of Benin, Benin - City, Nigeria.

www.ingramcontent.com/pod-product-compliance
Lightning Source LLC
Chambersburg PA
CBHW070906160726
48004CB00003B/1263